P9-DYY-399

THE GENIUS FILES

LICENSE TO THRILL

DAN GUTMAN

THE GENIUS FILES

LICENSE TO THRILL

HARPER

An Imprint of HarperCollinsPublishers

Library of Congress Cataloging-in-Publication Data
Gutman, Dan.
    License to thrill / Dan Gutman.
      pages cm. — (The Genius Files ; #5)
    Summary: "Tween twins Coke and Pepsi McDonald have finally
reached the last leg of their wacky and dangerous cross-country
road trip, but they must fend off a host of strange assassins before
they reach their home in California"— Provided by publisher.
    ISBN 978-0-06-223632-6
    [1. Adventure and adventurers—Fiction. 2. Genius—Fiction.
3. Brothers and sisters—Fiction. 4. Twins—Fiction. 5. Assassins—
Fiction. 6. Recreational vehicles—Fiction. 7. Family life—Fiction.]
    I. Title.
PZ7.G9846Li 2015   2014022043
[Fic]—dc23   CIP
                                                                        AC

Art and typography by Erin Fitzsimmons
15 16 17 18   CG/RRDH   10 9 8 7 6 5 4 3
❖
First Edition

Thanks to all the folks who helped me write this series: Laura Arnold, Mona Banton of the National Jousting Association, Jim Beard, Gail Bell, Brooke Bessesen, Peter and Jason Blau, Jane Sturdivant Britt, Steve Busti, Trish Carlberg, Diana Carr, Lisa Chapman, Edward Cheslek, Linda Clover, Joyce Allen-Crawford, Robert W. Dye, Christine Feller, Dennis Geoffroy, Esther Goldenberg, Google Maps, Sam and Emma Gutman, Ralph Hammelbacher, Jody Hotchkiss, Karen and Katie Jergensen, Robert Jones, Anne Kalkowski, Sarah Kaufman, Dave Kelly, Mary Kittrell, Alan and Samantha Kors, the Lucas family, Diandra Mae, Jennifer and Jabin Mallory, Sue Marchbanks, Elyse Marshall, Zack Medlin, P. J. Meriwether, Marcus and Jonathan Murdoch, Carrie O'Banion, Mike O'Connell, Dianne Odegard, Andrew and Lynne Paden, Jim Paillot, Andrea Reid, Shelley Riskin, Roadside America, Lara Robertson, Sarah Saladini, Kelly Salgado, John Shaffer of Luray Caverns, Angela Smith, Lucy and Jerry Trotta, Fred Valentini, Jon Van Hoozer Jr., and Jeremy Wolf.

Special thanks to my wife, Nina, who helped with all the art; my agent, Liza Voges; and Barbara Lalicki, Andrew Harwell, Rosemary Brosnan, and all the folks at HarperCollins. You make me look like a genius.

"Even the worst people in the world are
capable of changing, you know."
—*Nobody said this. But somebody should have.*

To the Reader . . .

All the places mentioned in this book are real.

You can visit them. You *should* visit them!

Well, maybe not the moon.

Cont

ents

Chapter 1

YOU'RE UP TO SPEED

There were eight items on Coke McDonald's to-do list at the end of July. But getting thrown into a volcano was not one of them.

GET A NEW IPOD was on the list.

STOP BITING MY NAILS was on the list.

BUY SCHOOL SUPPLIES was on the list.

FINISH SUMMER READING was on the list.

But nothing about getting thrown into a volcano.

And yet, strangely enough, getting thrown into a volcano was the *one* thing that Coke McDonald was actually going To Do at the end of July.

Dear reader, right here in the first chapter I could tell you how Coke McDonald is going to get thrown into a volcano. Then you would be able to get on with your life, go play a video game, watch some YouTube videos of cats playing piano, or whatever it is you do to get your jollies. But that would spoil the fun for you, and I certainly don't want to do that. Part of the joy of reading a book is letting the story unfold before your eyes. And to do that, you really need to read the first four books in the Genius Files series: *Mission Unstoppable*, *Never Say Genius*, *You Only Die Twice*, and *From Texas with Love*.

(By the way, these books are conveniently available in hardcover, paperback, ebook, and audiobook versions from your favorite bookseller. Or, if you're intent on depriving me of the piddling royalties I would earn if you actually *bought* the book, you can get it for *free* at your local library. You can't beat *that* deal.)

In any case, go ahead and read those four books. The rest of us will wait here while you catch up.

(insert whistling noises here)

Wait. What? You say you already *read* the first four Genius Files books? You say you remember that a pair of twins from California named Coke and Pepsi McDonald were recruited to be part of a secret government program called The Genius Files in which the smartest kids in the country would be called upon to solve the world's problems? You say you remember that the mastermind of The Genius Files program—the eccentric Dr. Herman Warsaw—decided to kill off the program and all the kids in it?

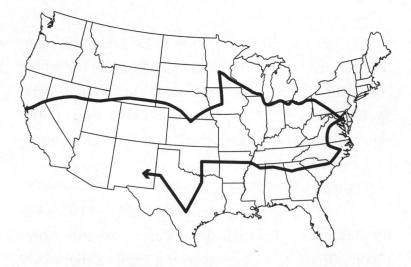

You say you already know that Dr. Warsaw, his deranged henchwoman Mrs. Higgins, Archie Clone, Evil Elvis, Doominator, and a pair of nincompoop flunkies wearing bowler hats have been chasing Coke and Pep across the United States all summer?

You say you remember that the twins jumped off a cliff, got locked in their burning school, were pushed into a sand pit and left to die, zapped with electric shocks, lowered into boiling oil in a giant french fry machine, run down by a remote-controlled car, kidnapped on a roller coaster, dipped in soft-serve ice cream while tied up in a Mister Softee truck, swarmed by a million flying bats, pushed into a spinning clothes dryer, poisoned through their bowling shoes, and had a cow dropped on their head?

(Deep breath)

You say you remember that Coke and Pep's clueless parents had no idea what was going on the whole time, thinking they were simply taking a wholesome family vacation? You say you remember some of the oddball tourist destinations the family visited along the way, such as . . .

(Deep breath)

. . . the Largest Ball of Twine in the World (Cawker City, Kansas), the Duct Tape Capital of the World (Avon, Ohio), the Largest Frying Pan in the World (Rose Hill, North Carolina), the National Bowling Hall of Fame (Arlington, Texas), the factory where Snickers are made (Waco, Texas), and museums devoted to Spam, Pez dispensers, hot dog buns, yo-yos, and my personal favorite, the Toilet Seat Art Museum (near San Antonio)?

You say you remember the shocking, blow-your-doors-off, didn't-see-that-coming climactic ending to *The Genius Files: From Texas with Love*, when Coke and Pep were playing ping-pong outside a motel in Roswell, New Mexico, and an alien spaceship landed and lifted the twins off the ground in a beam of bright light? You remember all that?

(Deep breath)

Oh.

Well, in that case, you're fully up to speed.

Splendid! Now we can plunge right ahead into the next installment of our story without having to go through all the boring rehash of what happened up to this point. That saves me a lot of time and effort.

Don't you hate when authors spend the whole first chapter of a book describing what happened in the *last* book of the series? I know I do.

Now all you need to do is sit back, munch on some cheesy chips or whatever unhealthy, fat-filled treat you favor, and enjoy *The Genius Files: License to Thrill*.

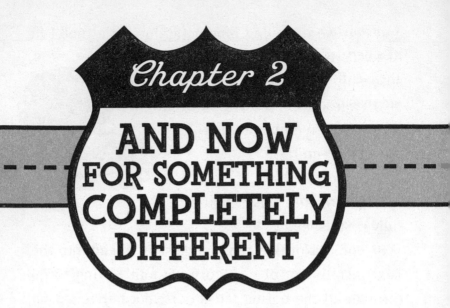

Chapter 2

AND NOW FOR SOMETHING COMPLETELY DIFFERENT

Pep felt her body rising slowly off the ground. Some mysterious, invisible force was gently lifting her up, as if she were filled with helium. She gripped her brother's hand tightly, so tightly that she was crushing his fingers together. But he didn't even notice the pain.

The twins had their eyes shut tightly, but the bluish glare from two powerful beams of light managed to penetrate their eyelids. The temperature had suddenly dropped twenty degrees. But Coke and Pep didn't feel it. The wind whipped at their clothes. A humming sound was coming from above, and the air seemed to vibrate around them. There was an odor they had never experienced before. Metallic, maybe. Impossible to describe. Powerful.

It was too much stimulation at one time. They couldn't move. They couldn't get away. They didn't *want* to get away. It was frightening, of course. But also magical. Intriguing.

"What's happening?" Pep whispered in wonder, fighting the temptation to open her eyes. She was afraid of being blinded by the light, or perhaps she was just afraid of seeing something she didn't want to see.

"I don't know," Coke replied. "But it's . . . *amazing!*"

Curiosity had gotten the better of him, as it often did, and Coke forced his eyes open. He involuntarily opened his mouth too as he hovered fifteen feet off the ground. He let out a little gasp. *This can't be happening*, he thought.

Months earlier, at the lunch table in school, he and his friends had had a heated discussion about which superpower they would choose if they could pick just one. One boy said he would love to have super vision so he could see through walls, and clothes. Another said he would choose super strength so he could beat up anybody in the world. Coke knew which superpower he would choose—the power to *fly*.

"We're *flying*," he marveled to his sister. "This is what it must feel like to be a bird."

"Where does the power come from?" Pep asked.

"Who cares?" he replied. "It's *beautiful*."

She finally opened her eyes too, and her retinas were clobbered by blasts of light coming at her from every direction. Yet she and Coke seemed to be enclosed within a narrow cylinder of air, as if they were going up a glass elevator shaft with no elevator inside it.

"ROY G BIV," Coke said, looking all around.

"Who's that?"

"Red, orange, yellow, green, blue, indigo, violet," Coke replied. "ROY G BIV. It's a mnemonic device people use to learn the colors of the rainbow, in order of decreasing wavelengths."

"Oh, yeah," Pep said, remembering her fifth-grade science class. "*Richard of York Gave Battle in Vain. Rinse Out Your Granny's Boots in Vinegar.* It's VIB-GYOR backward. That's how *I* remember it."

"Look at all the colors!" Coke said. "There are frequencies of light that I've never experienced before. Do you see 'em? *Wonderful* colors! They don't exist in our spectrum. They don't exist in our world."

"I see 'em," Pep said, looking all around. "I see 'em."

And then, suddenly, the lights went out. The twins were in total darkness.

⚜

"Who turned out the lights?" Coke asked, knowing full well that his sister had no idea who turned out the lights.

"I'm scared," Pep said, gripping her brother's hand even more tightly. "I have a bad feeling about this."

The darkness—the blackness—was total. There were no pinpricks of light scattered about. It felt like they must be indoors. They must have entered *something*. But there were no slits under a doorway where outside light could sneak through. Nothing. Their eyes were not going to adjust to the dark. There was nothing to adjust to. It was a power outage. A blackout. It was like all the light in the world had suddenly been switched off.

"What's happening?" Pep asked, just to make sure her brother was still there.

"Your guess is as good as mine."

"Maybe we were blinded," Pep said, shivering. "Maybe those lights wiped out our retinas, like an eraser on a whiteboard. Maybe we'll be blind *forever*."

And deaf? Coke wondered. The silence was

overwhelming. The humming noises were gone. There was no wind, no rustling of leaves in the trees, no chirping of birds. The twins could hear only the sound of their breathing. Pep thought she could detect her own heartbeat. But that was because it was beating very hard, and very fast.

She began to sob softly. Coke put his arm around her.

"Shhhh," he said. "We're gonna be okay."

It was wishful thinking.

Coke realized, an instant before his sister did, that he was no longer floating. His feet were on a surface now, and he could support his own weight. The floor must have come up from under them. He let go of Pep's hand and got down on his knees.

"It's soft," he whispered. "I can push my thumb into it and it springs back. It's sort of rubbery. Spongy. Like a padded playground."

"Let's get out of here," Pep whimpered. "I want to go back to the motel. Back to Mom and Dad."

"We've got to find the edge," Coke said, feeling around on the ground. "It must end somewhere. Maybe there's a door."

Pep had no choice but to get down on the floor with him. Coke was all she had, and she couldn't risk losing him.

"I have the feeling that somebody's watching us," she whispered.

"No time for your feelings," her brother replied, irritated. "The sooner we find the edge, the sooner we get out of here."

After a few minutes of crawling around, Coke *did* find an edge, a spot where the floor met a wall that seemed vertical, or close to it. He moved his hands up the wall, feeling around for a window or the crack of a door, but it was perfectly smooth and cold to the touch. He got back down on his knees so he could follow the wall around. It seemed like the room they were in was a large circle, maybe twenty or twenty-five feet in diameter.

"I feel something!" Pep suddenly shouted.

Coke crawled over to his right about ten feet, and he felt it too—vertical bars extending from the floor to as high as he could reach. They were made of some kind of metallic substance, about as thick as a salt shaker, and spaced five or so inches apart. The bars were too close together to squeeze through.

"It's like a cage," Coke said, gripping the bars and trying to shake them. "We're locked in."

"Like prisoners in jail," Pep said.

"Or animals in a zoo," her brother added.

That's when the lights flashed on, for just a

millisecond or two. It was a familiar white light this time, but painfully bright. Both twins covered their eyes with their hands. But for one split second, they were looking through the bars.

And in that split second, Pep glimpsed the alien.

Chapter 3

I'LL BELIEVE IT WHEN I SEE IT

Now, those of you who have been following the Genius Files know that I don't particularly like to describe what characters look like. For one thing, it's boring. Nobody wants to read page after page about somebody's face.

For another thing, if you have a short attention span like many of us do, you probably forget what characters look like five minutes after you read the description. That's why it doesn't say what Coke and Pep look like in *any* of these books.

You want to know what the twins look like? Look

at the book covers! There they are, jumping off a cliff, diving out of a boat or a helicopter. And if you want to know what Dr. Warsaw, Mrs. Higgins, the bowler dudes, or any of the other characters look like, *use your imagination*. That's what it's there for.

Having said all that, rules are meant to be broken. And this seems like the perfect time to break one.

You probably have a mental image of what a space alien looks like. You've seen hundreds of them in schlocky movies, TV shows, commercials, comic books, and so on. They're usually green, for some unknown reason, and they have these enormous, bulbous heads that are way out of proportion to their ridiculously skinny bodies. They never seem to have any hair, and they just stand there with emotionless, creepy-looking, almond-shaped eyes. They move in slow motion, if they move at all.

Well, just because somebody in Hollywood decided that aliens should look like that doesn't mean that's what they *really* look like. No, when Pep opened her eyes and glimpsed the alien for the first time, she saw a creature that was completely different from what she expected.

Picture this . . .

A round, doughy creature, about the size of a portable refrigerator. It had very small legs and feet with no pinky toes. At the end of each arm was a "hand" that was sort of a cross between a claw and a pair of pliers. The alien was wearing some sort of robe that changed color every few seconds.

The alien's face was a wonder to behold. It had two eyes (which shouldn't be taken for granted outside our solar system), but they were *red*. The eyes popped out slightly from the head, and they were all the more noticeable because the creature did not have any visible eyebrows or eyelashes. Or eyelids, for that matter. The eyes could not be closed, which made them even more frightening.

Its nose looked much like ours, but the alien had a wide, lipless, sunken mouth with one golden tooth in the middle. The other teeth appeared to have hair on them.

The alien had no external ears.

Unlike your typical Hollywood alien, this one had hair on its head—a patch of yellow-, black-, orange-, and red-patterned hair that glowed in the dark.

The skin, if you could call it skin, was reddish and translucent—much like fish scales. It appeared to be slimy to the touch, if one were to be so inclined to reach out and touch it.

Got all that? A few pages from now you'll probably forget the description, which is fine. Just remember this—it was a *hideous*-looking creature.

"*Ahhhhhhhhhhhhhhhhh!*" Pep shrieked.

It was a scream that seemed to go on forever. If the twins had not been confined inside a sealed, sound-proof enclosure, Pep would have been heard for miles in each direction.

Everything went dark again.

"Did you see *that*?"

"No, see what?" her brother replied. "I was facing the other way."

"It was like . . . an alien. Or something."

"You're hallucinating," Coke told his sister.

"I saw him!" Pep insisted. "Or it. Or whatever it was. It must have taken a picture of us with that flash of light."

"There's no such thing as aliens," Coke scoffed.

"Oh, I suppose we just got sucked up off the ground in Roswell, New Mexico, by a mysterious light that doesn't exist in our color spectrum, and aliens had nothing to do with it?"

"I'll believe it when I see it with my own eyes," Coke said firmly.

At that moment the light flashed on again, and this time it stayed on.

"*Ahhhhhhhhhhhhhhhhh!*" Coke and Pep shrieked simultaneously. Instinctively, they clung to each other for dear life. They were shaking, shivering. Their hearts were beating rapidly.

The alien didn't move, or make a sound, or react in any way.

"D-do you believe me *now*?" Pep asked, staring at the thing. "You're crushing my neck!"

Still terrified, Coke relaxed his grip on his sister, never taking his eyes off the creature on the other side of the bars.

"Did you ever hear of the Fermi Paradox?" he whispered.

"Of course not," Pep whispered back. "Only nerds like you know stuff like that."

Coke ignored that remark. The alien hadn't moved.

"Our galaxy has been around for billions of years," Coke whispered. "And there are billions of stars like our sun in the galaxy. And a lot of those stars must have Earth-like planets circling around them. So the Fermi Paradox asks, 'Where is everybody?' With all those billions of planets out there capable of supporting life, humans have never seen evidence of extraterrestrial life."

"Until now," Pep whispered, staring at the alien.

"I always said I wouldn't believe in anything that I couldn't see with my own eyes," Coke whispered. "But now I see it."

The creature had yet to make a move. It almost seemed like a statue. The twins' heartbeats slowed down just a little. The longer the creature sat there without doing anything, the less threatening it seemed.

"Do you think it's alive?" Pep whispered. "Maybe it's dead."

"Or maybe it's just watching us, and listening to us," Coke said softly. "Examining us."

"I doubt it can comprehend our language," Pep said, giving a little wave with her hand before speaking directly to the alien. "My name is Pep. This is my brother. His name is Coke. This is my head. This is called a nose. These are my ears."

She was speaking very clearly and slowly as she pointed to each body part, as if she was trying to communicate with someone from a foreign country. The alien had no reaction. Its eyes did not move.

"Don't waste your breath," Coke told her. "He doesn't understand English. Who even knows if he perceives sound waves the way we do?"

"How do you even know it's a *he*?" Pep asked. "Maybe she's a girl."

"No woman could be that ugly," Coke replied. "Anyway, maybe he has some other way of communicating. Or maybe he doesn't communicate at all."

"*All* living creatures communicate," Pep said. "At least the living creatures on Earth do."

"Hey, stupid!" Coke suddenly shouted at the alien. "Do you understand me *now*? You're a moron, you know that? An idiot! You don't have any brains!"

"Stop it!" Pep warned her brother. "If he *does* understand anything, you're going to make him mad."

"So what?" Coke said. "Let him get mad! At least then he'll react. This guy is boring. Talking to this guy is like talking to a brick wall. Why don't you say something, you jerk! You're a dope! *Do* something! See, he doesn't understand a word I'm saying."

At that moment, the creature's lipless, sunken mouth opened ever so slightly. A sound came out.

"Flog slab," it said.

Chapter 4
FLOG SLAB

"**D**id you hear *that*?" Pep said excitedly. "He *spoke*!"

"I didn't hear anything," Coke said. "What did he say?"

"It sounded like *frog slab*," Pep said, "or something like that."

"Flog slab," repeated the alien.

"He said it *again*!" Pep shouted.

"It's not *frog slab*," said her brother. There was an *L* sound in there. Like, *flog sllllllab*."

The twins tried to figure out what *flog slab* could possibly mean.

"Maybe *flog slab* is his *name*," Pep guessed. "Flog Slab. It's kinda cute, actually."

"That's a pretty weird name," Coke said.

"Well, what do you expect an alien from another planet to be named?" asked his sister. "Bob?"

"We haven't established with certainty that he's from another planet," Coke told her. "He could be in disguise. This could all be a hoax. Maybe we're in the middle of some reality TV show. They just want to freak us out to get a reaction."

"So as I was saying," Pep said to the alien. "My name is Pep. Pepsi McDonald, to be specific. We're twins. We're thirteen years old. We live in California. We're on a cross-country trip."

Coke looked around to see if there might be a camera crew hiding behind him. As he did, two more aliens came out of the shadows and positioned themselves on either side of the first alien. One was slightly bigger than the first one, and one was slightly smaller. Other than that, they looked similar.

"Ahhhhhhhhhhhhhhhhhhh!" Pep shrieked. "There are *three* of them!"

She leaped into her brother's arms and hid her face so she wouldn't have to look at them.

"Flog slab," said all three aliens. They stared at the

twins with piercing red eyes.

"I don't like this!" Pep moaned, tears running down her cheeks. "They've got us outnumbered now. I want to get out of here."

"Flog slab," said the first alien.

"Flog slab," said the second alien.

"Flog slab," said the third alien.

"Maybe they're a family," Coke said, trying to look on the bright side.

"And maybe the family is going to kill us!" Pep shouted. "Maybe they're going to do bizarre medical experiments on us first, and *then* kill us."

"You watch too many science fiction movies," Coke said. "Maybe they're friendly."

"Let us go!" Pep shouted at the aliens. "Let us out of this place!"

"We mean no harm," Coke said, holding his hands up and making a *V* sign with his fingers. "Let us live in peace."

"Flog slab flog slab flog slab," chanted the aliens.

The aliens droned on and on. Coke closed his eyes and put his hands over his ears in a desperate attempt to block out the sound.

"Stop saying that!" he hollered. "They're driving me crazy! It's some form of mind control! Make it stop!"

"Flog slab flog slab flog slab flog slab flog slab flog

slab flog slab flog slab flog slab flog slab flog slab flog slab flog slab."

The aliens appeared to be excited now, as if they had made some connection with the two Earth children behind the bars. Their chanting picked up a little speed. There was urgency in it. It continued droning on in the background as Coke and Pep tried to figure out what they should do.

"*Flog slab* probably doesn't mean *anything*," Coke guessed. "Maybe it's just a random noise they make. Like cows moo, cats meow, ducks quack, and these guys flog slab."

"Flog slab flog slab flog slab flog slab flog slab flog slab flog slab flog slab flog slab."

The chanting was getting louder and more insistent. Each of the three aliens was saying "flog slab" in a slightly different tone, creating a haunting, harmonic effect that served to calm the twins' nerves and put them into an almost hypnotic state.

It had been a long day, and now it was getting late. Coke and Pep were exhausted from their experience, and the droning sound of "flog slab" was like a mantra. A spell. After a short period of time, both of them lay their heads on the floor, closed their eyes, and fell into a deep slumber.

As soon as the twins were asleep, the three aliens stopped chanting and scurried around on their little feet. One of them opened the bars that had separated them from Coke and Pep. The others wheeled in two long, metal tables. Seemingly with no effort, they lifted Coke and Pep onto the tables and rolled them into the next room.

It was an amazing place—there was a wall made from hundreds of video screens of every size, from postage stamp to big-screen TV. There were no knobs, dials, or switches anywhere, like you would expect in a high-tech hospital or airplane cockpit. Every screen was controlled by touching it, which the aliens did with amazing dexterity and speed.

In the middle of the room was a large, white machine that resembled the devices hospitals use to shoot magnetic resonance images of patients. It was, in fact, very much like an MRI machine, but much, *much* more powerful. While the twins slept, the tables they lay on were wheeled into this machine. One of the aliens touched a screen on the wall, and a purplish band of light shone on Coke, then Pep. The light, accompanied by an otherworldly humming sound, traveled up and down their bodies like a scanner or photocopy machine. Then it stopped and repeated the procedure a second time, in the opposite direction.

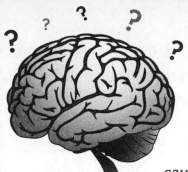

For centuries, scientists have been trying to unlock the mysteries of the human brain. Why are some people "smarter" than others? What causes autism, dyslexia, and other learning disabilities? They want to find out what makes us "tick." It's as if our brains were the innards of an old grandfather clock, and we could watch and see how the gears, wheels, and complicated mechanisms ultimately make the clock's hands go around.

Just one little problem: The human brain is made of eighty-five to a hundred *billion* neurons and neural pathways. They're constantly growing, changing, and dying off. It would take three *petabytes* of storage to capture the amount of information generated by just one *million* neurons in a year. The brain generates 300,000 petabytes of data each year.

Even with the powerful computers we have, our best neuroscientists haven't come close to figuring out exactly how the human brain functions. It's far more complicated than sequencing the human genome.

Someday, perhaps in your lifetime, it will be possible to record every single neuron in the brain and create a comprehensive BAM—brain activity map. Scientists will be able to peer inside a person's head and see exactly what he or she is thinking, feeling, and planning at any moment in time. It might be as easy as taking an X-ray, or glancing at your smartphone.

The aliens, possessing a far more sophisticated intelligence than our own, had figured out a way to reverse-engineer the human brain. They knew how to use powerful lasers and nano-robots to measure the activity of neurons in a brain's cortex. They learned how to create and connect billions of virtual neurons together in a network of simulated waves that worked just like a real brain. And once they had mastered that, they sent these three ambassadors to Earth to see if it worked on humans.

Using a technology we can't even begin to understand, the three hideous-looking creatures installed a virtual "sensor mesh" of 364 electrodes on the surface of Coke's and Pep's brain. Upon the touch of a screen, the information was extracted, copied, and analyzed. Coke and Pep didn't feel a thing. Their skin was never broken.

While the twins slept, a complete map of their brains was downloaded into the alien computer system.

It took about thirty seconds.

Chapter 5

COKE'S NIGHTMARE

At this point, you're probably wondering when Coke is going to get thrown into a volcano. Be patient, dear reader. Good things come to those who wait. We're only in chapter 5.

While Coke slept, the neurons in his brain kept firing. The result was a dream that was almost like a movie in his head. It looked like this . . .

🦌

Beautiful summer day. Coke and Pep were floating on inflatable pool rafts in the middle of a lake. There were no boats in sight. They didn't have a care in the world.

Then, suddenly, the peace was disturbed by a faraway noise—the sound of a motor, possibly a small boat. Coke looked up. In the distance, he could see two tiny dots.

"What's going on?" Pep asked.

"Sounds like motorboats."

But the dots were *not* motorboats. They were Jet Skis. And they were heading directly toward the twins.

Pep waved her arms to signal the drivers. But they didn't seem to notice.

"I don't have a good feeling about this," Pep said.

As the Jet Skis drew closer, the twins could see that two men were driving them. Two men wearing bowler hats.

"Bowler dudes at twelve o'clock!" Coke shouted.

"They're gonna run us down!" Pep screamed.

"Jump!" Coke shouted.

He could see the bowler dudes' faces, snickering and giggling like idiots. He took a deep gulp of air and dove off his raft at the last possible instant before the Jet Ski would have rammed him. It passed right over, ripping the raft to shreds. Coke struggled to swim back to the surface.

"Oooh, missed him by *that* much!" cackled the mustachioed bowler dude.

"This is *fun*!" shouted his clean-shaven brother. "We should do water sports more often!"

As Coke's head bobbed above the surface, he saw Pep, treading water and gasping for breath. Her raft had also been destroyed.

"They're trying to kill us!" she shouted.

The Jet-Skiing bowler dudes were circling around, gunning their engines for another attack.

"They're coming back!" Pep screamed.

"Get underwater!" Coke shouted, before filling his lungs with air.

The bowler dudes came roaring back, aiming their Jet Skis for the two heads bobbing in the water. Once again, the twins dove below the surface at the last second, avoiding certain death.

"It's like Whac-A-Mole, but with people!" shouted the clean-shaven bowler dude as he passed by the spot where Pep's head had been a moment earlier.

Coke and Pep stayed underwater as long as they could hold their breath. When they surfaced, a large yacht was approaching from the west. It cruised to a stop. There was a woman standing at the rail.

"Mrs. Higgins!" Coke shouted.

Yes, it was Mrs. Audrey Higgins, their germaphobic health teacher. She reached a hand down for Coke and Pep to climb aboard the yacht, and gave each of them a towel.

"You saved our lives!" Pep marveled. "Why? You *hate* us. You've been trying to kill us ever since you locked us in the detention room and burned the school down."

"Well, I didn't want *those* idiots to kill you," Mrs. Higgins replied matter-of-factly, "because I wanted to do it *myself*!"

It took a moment for Mrs. Higgins's words to sink in. It also took a moment for the colorless, sweet-smelling liquid she had soaked the towels in to take effect. But very soon, Coke and Pep were feeling lightheaded.

"What's that smell?" Coke asked.

"I think . . . I'm going to . . . pass out," said Pep.

"It's my favorite scent—chloroform," said Mrs. Higgins. "It increases the movement of potassium ions through the nerve cells, which serves to depress your central nervous system. The result will be cardiac arrhythmia. Don't worry, in a few minutes you won't smell a thing. Because you'll be *dead*."

Clearly, she was insane.

Unbeknownst to Mrs. Higgins, a helicopter had

landed at the other side of her yacht. While she was busy poisoning the twins with chloroform, the helicopter pilot—a red-haired teenager—had come running over.

"Step aside, you old hag!" he said, shoving Mrs. Higgins overboard.

"Archie Clone!" Pep yelled.

Yes, it was Archie Clone, the teenage supervillain who had attempted to drop them onto the tip of the Washington Monument.

"Come with me!" Archie Clone yelled. "Quickly!"

"I thought you died in Washington!" Coke yelled as he and Pep ran and climbed into the passenger side of the helicopter. It had no door on it.

"You thought wrong," Archie Clone replied. He grabbed the controls and the chopper lifted off the yacht.

Archie Clone turned the helicopter and pointed it toward the edge of the lake. Soon the twins could see land passing below. Archie Clone slowed the chopper and hovered over what appeared to be a junkyard. He descended to ten feet. The twins couldn't see what was below.

"Pep, I've had a crush on you for a long time," Archie Clone shouted. "Now, finally, I have the opportunity to express my feelings toward you."

With that, he stuck his foot out to the side and pushed both twins out of the helicopter.

"Hellllllllp!" they shouted as they landed in the dirt inside a four-walled enclosure that looked like it was made from iron. When the helicopter flew away and the dust had cleared, they could see a familiar figure standing at the top of one of the iron walls.

"Evil Elvis!" Coke shouted.

Yes, it was Evil Elvis, the Presley impersonator also known as their aunt Judy. He—that is, she—had terrorized them all the way from North Carolina to Tennessee.

"We thought you died in the RV explosion!" Pep said.

"Elvis *never* dies," said Evil Elvis.

Suddenly, a grinding noise could be heard. The twins could see that the walls of the iron enclosure were moving together. The space was getting smaller.

"What's happening?" Coke yelled.

"Oh, don't worry your little head about it," said Evil Elvis. "This is just a machine they use to crush old cars."

"So *that's* what Archie Clone meant when he said he had a crush on you," Coke told his sister.

Coke took a running leap at the iron wall, but it was

too high to climb over. He fell to the ground and had to scramble to back away.

The iron walls continued closing in on all sides. The enclosure had shrunk from the size of a large living room to the size of a bathroom.

"Ha-ha!" shouted Evil Elvis. "Finally, I'll be finished with you twerps! When these walls come together, you will be crushed to death. Your bones will break like twigs and your internal organs will burst like water balloons!"

"Why are you doing this?" Pep screamed frantically. "You're our mother's sister!"

"I'm doing it for Dr. Warsaw," Aunt Judy/Evil Elvis said solemnly. "The man I love."

Speak of the devil! Guess who suddenly appeared standing on the other moving wall?

"Dr. Warsaw!" shouted Coke.

"No, it's *me*, Doominator!"

It's true. It was Doominator, the robot clone Dr. Warsaw had created to duplicate himself. He looked and sounded identical to the *real* Dr. Warsaw.

The walls continued closing in on the twins. The sides were less than ten feet apart now. Pep screamed.

"I thought you drowned in the log flume pool!" Coke shouted. "I saw it with my own eyes!"

"That robot *did* drown," Doominator replied. "I'm

an exact copy of him. I am . . . Doominator 2."

"You're a clone of a clone?" Coke asked.

"That's right," Doominator 2 said. "The beauty of digital information is that copies can be made at the touch of a button."

"I don't care if you're a clone!" shouted Aunt Judy/ Evil Elvis. "I love you anyway."

"Yeah, well I don't love *you*," Doominator 2 said. "Leave those kids alone!"

He ran over and the next thing anyone knew, the two of them were fighting at the top of the iron wall.

"Don't be cruel!" Aunt Judy/Evil Elvis shouted just before Doominator 2 caught her with a forearm to the face. She fell backward and out of sight.

"Elvis has left the building!" said Doominator 2.

With Aunt Judy/Evil Elvis dispatched, Doominator 2 jumped into the pit with the twins. They recoiled in horror, imagining the next unspeakable thing that was going to happen to them. But instead of raising an arm against them, Doominator 2 got down on the ground in the middle of the moving walls.

"I'm made of iron," Doominator 2 said. "These walls will not be able to crush me. It's impossible."

Sure enough, when the walls reached his head and feet, they pressed against him with a huge amount of force, but the robot clone didn't collapse. The moving walls abruptly stopped. The noisy gears ground to a halt.

"You saved our lives!" Pep shouted.

"Don't mention it," Doominator 2 grunted. "Run! Get away from here, as far as you can go. Climb on top of me to get out!"

The twins were about to use Doominator 2 as a stepstool, but at that moment somebody climbed in and grabbed them roughly from behind.

"Going somewhere?"

"Dr. Warsaw!" Coke and Pep yelled simultaneously.

Yes, it was Dr. Herman Warsaw. The *real*, *human* Dr. Herman Warsaw, who had created The Genius Files program and become psychotic as a result of 9/11. He had been trying to kill off the twins ever since they were home in California. As always, a cigarette dangled from his lips.

"That just goes to show that if you want something done right, do it yourself," Dr. Warsaw spat. "Enough incompetence! Why must I be surrounded by idiots?"

"Coke! Do something!"

But there was nothing anyone could do. Dr. Warsaw reached into his jacket and pulled out a pistol.

"No more gimmicks," he said. "From now on we do things the old-fashioned way."

"Please! Please!" Coke said. "We'll do anything you ask."

"Stop begging," Dr. Warsaw said. "You're pathetic."

"No! Don't!"

He pulled the trigger.

Chapter 6

ENGLISH AS A SECOND LANGUAGE

"Coke, wake up!" Pep shouted in her brother's ear.

"Huh? What?"

Her brother bolted up and shook his head, as if that would erase the bad thoughts from his brain.

"I was having a dream," he said, still fuzzy. "A nightmare."

"About what?"

"We were floating on rafts in a lake," Coke recalled, "and then the bowler dudes tried to run us down with Jet Skis . . . but we were rescued by Mrs. Higgins . . .

and then she tried to kill us with chloroform . . . but we were saved by Archie Clone . . . and then *he* tried to kill us in a giant car-crushing machine . . . and then Evil Elvis and Doominator showed up. And then Dr. Warsaw. They were *all* trying to do horrible things to us!"

Pep motioned for her brother to look to the left, where the three aliens were staring at them intently. It didn't take a genius to realize that the situation he was currently in was not a whole lot better than his nightmare. Coke flinched.

"Flog slab," said the alien across the room.

"Stop saying that!" Coke shouted, getting up off the table he had been lying on. "Is that all you know how to say?"

"Flog slab," said the alien in the middle.

The twins both had slight headaches, but didn't realize it was because their brains had been probed. They glanced quickly around the room. All the screens and unusual equipment made it look like a hospital, or perhaps some kind of a laboratory.

"Do you think they performed bizarre medical experiments on us while we were sleeping?" Pep asked. She examined her arms and legs for cuts, scars, or bruises, but found nothing.

"I don't know," Coke replied. "Why don't you ask

Moe, Larry, and Curly over there?"

"Flog slab," said the alien on the right.

"You know what?" Coke said. "I've had enough of you three."

"What did you *do* to us?" Pep begged the aliens. "Why are we here? When will you let us go? We want to go back to our parents."

"You're wasting your breath," her brother told her. "They're not going to answer. All they know how to say is *flog slab.*"

"Boolay," said the one he'd called Moe. "Boolay wow boolay."

Coke and Pep looked at each other, then back at the three aliens. Pep's jaw dropped open.

"What did you say?" she asked.

"Boolay wow boolay," said Larry, nodding its head.

"Boolay wow boolay," said Curly.

"Gurk quizzlibub," said Moe. "Gurk quizzlibub good evening gurk quizzlibub."

"They're *talking*!" Coke exclaimed. "They're using words that sound something like our words. What do they mean?"

"I don't know," Pep said, "but I'm going to figure it out."

Pep loved word games and she was excellent at solving puzzles of all kinds. To a large extent, her verbal skill was the reason why she and Coke were still alive. If she hadn't been able to figure out all those ciphers along the road, there was no telling what would have happened to them.

Pep faced the aliens and slowly asked, "What does *boolay* mean?"

"Boolay wow boolay," said Moe, who appeared to be the "spokesman" for the group. "Boolay wow boolay wow."

"Wait a minute. Does *boolay* mean 'wow'?" Pep asked.

"Boolay wow boolay wow," all three aliens responded, nodding their heads vigorously. "Gurk quizzlibub good evening gurk quizzlibub."

"*Boolay* means 'wow' in their language!" Pep said, jumping up and down. "Boolay!"

"Boolay wow boolay," said Curly.

"You don't know that for sure," Coke told his sister. "Maybe they're just making random vocalizations, or imitating you. Like a parrot or something."

"Boolay boolay boolay," said the aliens.

"Gurk quizzlibub good evening gurk quizzlibub," said the one the twins had dubbed Larry.

"Do you think *gurk quizzlibub* means 'good evening'?" Pep asked. "Maybe *gurk* means 'good' and *quizzlibub* means 'evening.'"

"Don't look at *me*," Coke said, "I don't speak alien."

"Gurk quizzlibub good evening," said Curly. "Good evening gurk quizzlibub."

"Yes! Yes! Yes!" Pep shouted, clapping her hands.

"Yerp yes yerp yes yerp yes," said Moe.

"And *yerp* must mean 'yes'!" Pep said. "Can you believe this? We're communicating with them!"

"It sounds as if we can say any English word and they'll translate it," Coke said.

"Hand," Pep said, holding up her hand for the aliens to see.

"Blisky," said the aliens. "Blisky hand. Hand blisky."

"Eyes," Pep said, pointing to her eyes.

"Klimps," said the aliens. "Klimps eyes. Eyes klimps."

"Nose," Pep said, touching her nose.

"Snorfle," said the aliens. "Snorfle nose. Nose snorfle."

"Spy," said Coke, wanting to get in on the conversation.

"Snarg," said the aliens. "Snarg spy. Spy snarg."

"Love," Pep said, cradling her arms as if she was hugging herself.

"Zurk," said the aliens. "Zurk love. Love zurk."

Coke and Pep, excited at this breakthrough, moved closer to the three aliens. It was still a frightening situation, but the joy of communicating with beings from another planet had more than made up for any apprehension the twins had.

After translating all the major body parts, they advanced to more difficult words and concepts. Up/Down. Bad/Good. In/Out. Take. Make. Went. Give. Like. Go. Be. Have. Do. Say. And so on. Soon full sentences and quotations were shooting back and forth.

"To be or not to be, that is the question," said Pep.

"To zweek or blop to zweek, that is the snazzle wogger," Moe replied.

"Give me liberty or give me death," said Coke.

"Give me rendium or give me gogwatsfu," Larry replied.

"The rain in Spain falls mainly on the plain," said Coke.

"The okletoxx in Purzly derps mortrab on the flamplant," replied Moe.

"I think they've got it!" exclaimed Coke.

"I chukah fliff snix barble!" exclaimed Curly.

In a short period of time, the aliens were able to understand simple English and the twins had a working knowledge of the alien language. Suddenly, they looked like they were all old friends.

"Wait a minute," Coke said. "What about flog slab? What does *that* mean?"

"Flog slab golf balls flog slab golf balls flog slab golf balls," chanted the aliens.

"Wait a minute," Pep said. "Flog slab means golf balls? None of your *other* words were spelled backward. That doesn't make sense."

"English makes sense?" asked Moe. "Aren't you the ones who drive on the parkway and park on the driveway?"

"So, you understand English?" Pep finally asked the aliens.

"Yerp," replied Moe. "We do now. While the two of you were murkling—I mean sleeping—we examined your brains."

"You looked inside my sister's brain?" Coke asked. "Did you find anything?"

"Very funny, Coke," Pep said. "On our planet, we would call it an invasion of privacy. They could have done *anything* to us while we were asleep. Did you do bizarre medical experiments on us?"

"That depends on what you mean by bizarre," said Moe. "We learned how your skrats, I mean brains, generate thoughts, dreams, memories, perceptions, and other mental images. And we learned your language."

"Golf balls golf balls golf balls!" chanted Larry and Curly.

"Why do they keep saying golf balls?" Coke asked.

"Oh, you'll find out," said Moe.

"How long were we asleep?" Pep asked.

"About five splinks, I mean minutes," Moe said.

"You mean to say that in just five minutes you analyzed our brains and learned the entire English language?"

"No," said Moe. "We also had some wergle. I mean, lunch."

Pep was flabbergasted. She had taken a full year of French at school during the fourth grade, and she barely remembered anything beyond *bonjour* and *Où est la bibliothèque?* ("Where is the library?")

Coke was equally impressed, and a little intimidated. He had never met anyone who came *close* to his level of intelligence, much less surpassed it. Coke's IQ score, he knew, was in the mid-150 range, which qualified him as a genius. *The Guinness Book of World Records*, which he had memorized cover to cover, once listed a woman named Marilyn vos Savant with an IQ of 190, one of the highest ever recorded.

"What's your IQ?" Coke asked the aliens.

"Using your primitive method of measuring intelligence," said Moe, "our scores would be in the range of 650."

No longer fearful, Coke and Pep were fascinated by these strange, super-intelligent creatures from another world. What a unique opportunity to answer some of the questions mankind had been pondering for centuries. There were so many things to ask. So many things to know. How was the universe created? What is the purpose of life? But the most important question, of course, came first.

"Where are you from?" Pep asked.

"We are from the planet Kayaanga," Moe replied.

The twins were sitting among the aliens. Coke's knees were mere inches from those of Curly, but he had no fear. Just the opposite, really. He and his sister had obviously been abducted by these aliens who were in a position to do anything they wanted, and yet a sense of calm had come over both of the twins. They knew they were experiencing something that few—maybe nobody—in our world had ever witnessed. They would have some story to tell when they got home. That is, if they ever made it home.

It was quiet. Pep held her brother's hand.

"Well, it has been really great hanging out with you guys," Coke said, stretching as he got to his feet. "But we need to be heading back—"

"We have come to your planet for a reason," Moe said.

"Huh?" Pep asked. "I beg your pardon?"

A low rumbling sound could be heard below them.

"What's that?" Coke asked, sitting back down quickly. "What's happening?"

"Oh, it's nothing to worry about," said Moe. "We are about to flumphus, I mean blast off."

"Blast off?" Pep asked, squeezing her brother's hand tightly. "Where are we going?"

"You'll find out."

Chapter 7

LIFTOFF

The rumbling from below was accompanied by a loud humming noise, as if a billion cats were purring into microphones and the sound was being pumped out of speakers positioned all around. Gentle vibrations washed over Coke and Pep. They could feel the hair on their arms standing on end.

"This is a joke, right?" asked Coke.

"I suggest you strap into the seats over there, and quickly," warned Moe.

"But we have to *leave*!" Pep shouted. "Our parents are waiting for us back at the motel!"

"Too late for that now," Moe informed them. He and the other two aliens went off to busy themselves in preparation for liftoff.

If you've ever watched old videos of the Apollo missions or the space shuttles rising up off the launch pad, it looks like everything is moving in slow motion. It takes an incredible amount of fuel—and a lot of time—to escape the grip of the earth's gravity.

But this was not like that at all. Using an advanced propulsion technology that human rocket scientists can only dream about, the spaceship seemed to lift almost effortlessly off the ground and rise to treetop level. If the nation's sophisticated defense systems detected an unidentified flying object, nothing was done about it. No jets were scrambled. The president was not informed. Nobody in the area of Roswell, New Mexico, noticed anything unusual in the night sky.

In seconds, the ship was gliding on a straight vertical path, pushing the earth's atmosphere out of its way like it was strolling through a beaded curtain.

Of course, the effect on the human body was not so smooth. Newton's laws saw to that. As the ship went from zero to 17,500 miles per hour in less than four minutes, Coke and Pep felt themselves being pushed hard against the floor. Coke looked down to see the flesh on his legs pulling against the bones. If he could have seen the soft tissue of his cheeks flapping, he would have laughed.

"We must be pulling four g's," Coke groaned to nobody in particular.

It was five, actually.

The twins felt pressure across their chests as the ship punched its way through the troposphere. They felt heavy. It was like they had doubled their weight instantly.

There were two seats that looked like dentist chairs in the corner, and a large window in front of them. The twins struggled to crawl over to the chairs and strap themselves in.

"Look!" Coke said, pointing out the window.

Earth was falling away before their eyes. Coke, of course, remembered learning about the layers of the atmosphere in school. At seven and a half miles up, the troposphere ends and the stratosphere begins. At twenty-one miles, the stratosphere ends and the mesosphere begins. At around forty-nine miles, they reached the thermosphere.

Coke almost expected to see lines dividing the layers of air, the way they do in textbook graphs. But the real world was not so obvious. There were no borders separating each layer of the atmosphere. It just got ssively darker. By the time they reached the ere, outer space was inky black.

thing that struck Coke and Pep was how everything looked so *clear*. The stars didn't look like faraway, sparkly dots. They were so much brighter, like planets. They didn't twinkle; they glowed. There was no atmosphere to cloud one's vision.

"We're . . . astronauts," Pep said, marveling at the view of the earth from above.

"It's . . . beautiful," Coke said, gazing at the enormous blue marble with white swirling around it.

"So much water!" Pep said.

Her brother pointed out that the white swirls were clouds, ice, and snow. They could see the larger rivers, continents, and the lights of big cities. The earth seemed to get smaller as they rocketed away from it.

"Where's the equator?" Pep asked.

"The equator is an imaginary line, you dope," Coke said, without taking his eyes from the window. "It's not like there's a giant rubber band around the middle of the planet."

Pep gasped for a moment when she suddenly realized they would need helmets and spacesuits to survive the airless world of outer space. But there were no helmets or spacesuits within sight. Since they had not dropped dead yet, the twins came to the logical conclusion that the aliens were capable of breathing oxygen just like we do, and had been pumping it into the ship.

"Where do you think they're taking us?" Pep asked.

"To their home planet, I guess."

Pep's eyes felt watery and a single tear rolled down her cheek. She wiped it away with her sleeve. It was extremely possible that she would never see *her* home planet again.

"What do you think Mom and Dad are doing right now?" she asked.

"Sleeping," her brother replied. "Or maybe worrying about us."

"That's what I'm doing too," Pep replied.

"By now, they probably realize that we didn't come

back to the motel room," Coke said, after thinking it over more analytically. "After they look around and don't find us, they'll call the police and report us missing. The cops will show up with dogs to search the woods. That's what they do when kids disappear."

"But they won't find us," Pep said, wiping away another tear.

"They'll look all over," Coke said quietly. "After thirty days, the police don't call it a search and rescue mission anymore. It's a recovery mission. They figure they're not going to find anybody alive at that point. Then they start searching for bodies."

"They won't find bodies, either," Pep said. "They won't find *anything*. We will have just vanished into thin air."

"I wonder if *all* the kids who have vanished without a trace were abducted by aliens," Coke said. "That would explain a lot. Maybe they're *all* being held captive on this alien planet, Kayaanga. Maybe we'll meet them."

Pep wasn't thinking about other kids. She was thinking about herself, her brother, and her parents.

"I know we argue with them and make fun of Mom and Dad all the time," Pep said, sniffling, "but I really love them."

"Me too," Coke replied.

By this time, the earth had dropped away and the

ship turned so Coke and Pep couldn't see it anymore. All they could see was the blackness of space. The ship had stopped accelerating and was moving at a steady speed, so it seemed like it wasn't moving at all. The twins felt no pressure on their bodies. The aliens were off in another room.

"Y'know, we were better off before," Pep told her brother. "We were better off when all we had to worry about was Dr. Warsaw, Mrs. Higgins, and those stupid bowler dudes trying to kill us. At least we were on our own planet. At least we could *do* something. We could run. We could fight back. We can't do *anything* here. We're trapped."

"If we ever get out of this thing," Coke told his sister, "I promise I'll never complain about anything ever again."

"We're not going to get out of this," Pep said with a sigh. "We'll never come home."

It was true, they both realized. They would never see their parents, friends, teachers, or California ever again. They would never learn how to drive, or go to high school and college and experience all the other things kids experience as teenagers. They would never get married or have children of their own. Their lives were over, and there was nothing they could do about it.

Pep rested her head on her brother's shoulder and closed her eyes.

"I feel light-headed," she said.

"Me too," Coke replied.

At that moment, both twins opened their eyes wide as they came to the realization that they had escaped the gravitational pull of Earth. It wasn't that they were light-headed. Like any other object in outer space, they were *weightless*.

Coke unbuckled his seat belt. A grin spread across his face as his body slowly floated up off the seat. Pep unbuckled her seat belt as well. At first she was tentative, holding her arms unsteadily outstretched in an attempt to balance and keep herself upright. But soon she realized that it didn't matter if she was upside down, right side up, or sideways. In a matter of minutes, she was ping-ponging off the walls, floor, and ceiling alongside her brother.

"Woo-hoo!" Coke yelled. "I'm flying!"

For a brief moment, the twins forgot that they would never see their friends or family again. Weightlessness was irresistibly fun.

"Is this cool, or what?" Coke cackled as he bumped into Pep with a tangle of arms and legs. "Woo-hoo!"

"This must be what it's like to be a bird!" Pep said with a giggle.

They were having such a good time that neither of them noticed that their alien hosts—Moe, Larry, and Curly—had entered the room once again.

"I'd suggest you strap yourselves in," said Moe.

Coke and Pep pushed off the ceiling and wall in order to fly over toward the seats. It took a little maneuvering to turn their bodies around and put on their seat belts.

"Where are you taking us?" Coke demanded. "What are you going to do with us? We have the right to know."

"Yeah," Pep said, trying to sound as authoritative as her brother.

"Isn't it obvious?" asked Moe, pointing to the window.

Coke and Pep turned their heads and saw something they had seen thousands of times before, but never so large or so bright . . .

The moon.

Chapter 8

SWEEGLING IN SPACE

As the ship closed in, the moon just about filled the window. Its surface was silvery with millions of craters of all sizes, and dark and light patches of gray and brown. There were no other colors, but it was a beautiful thing nevertheless. Coke's and Pep's jaws dropped open as they gazed in wonder.

Decades ago, it took the Apollo astronauts about three days to travel 239,000 miles to the moon. In 2006, the NASA Pluto probe took a little over eight hours to get there. Onboard the alien spacecraft, Coke and Pep had made the trip in twenty-four minutes.

The moon may look like a perfect sphere from our vantage point, but it's not. As the ship got closer, the twins could see huge mountains and valleys.

"Approaching the Sea of Clouds," said Moe. "Steady as you go."

Curly and Larry busied themselves with the controls, which they carried in their clawlike hands. Coke and Pep couldn't tear their eyes away from the window.

"Only a few human beings have walked on the surface," Pep mused out loud.

"Twelve," Coke replied.

"How do you know that?"

"Doesn't everybody know that?" Coke asked, then reeled them off. "Armstrong, Aldrin, Conrad, Bean, Shepard, Mitchell, Irwin, Scott, Duke, Young, Schmitt, and Cernan."

"What possible reason did you have to memorize those names?" Pep asked.

"I didn't *try* to memorize them," Coke replied. "It just happened."

The ship was slowing down. The twins could feel the weightlessness wearing off. Through the window, they could see the surface more clearly now. Some of the craters had debris around the circles that fanned out in a pattern like rays of sunlight. Something must have hit the moon *hard* to create those. Coke informed his sister that one crater, called Clavius, was 146 miles wide.

"Prepare for landing," Moe announced.

"Why are they taking us *here*?" Pep whispered to her brother.

"Beats me."

As the ship descended to the surface, Coke spotted something familiar off in the distance—a lunar module that was used by our astronauts back in the 1970s. It had four "legs" and was partly covered with gold foil that stood out from all the black and white. It looked a little bit like a spider. There was other equipment strewn near the lunar module, and an American flag sticking in the surface of the moon.

"Look!" Coke said, pointing out the window. "It's the stuff left behind by one of the Apollo missions."

The ship touched down with a gentle *clunk* and the engine vibrations suddenly stopped. For a moment, all was silent.

"Flog slab," the aliens began to chant. "Flog slab. Flog slab."

"Oh no," Pep groaned. "Not with the *flog slab* again."

"*Flog slab* means 'golf balls,' remember?" Coke reminded her.

"So what?" Pep said. "What do golf balls have to do with the moon?"

Coke knew exactly what golf balls had to do with the moon. He had watched a TV documentary about it when he was in first grade.

It was all because of Alan Shepard, who was the first American in space, back in 1961. A decade later, in February of 1971, he became the fifth human being to walk on the moon, as a member of Apollo 14. When the mission was nearly complete, Shepard took two golf balls he had hidden in his space suit and dropped them on the surface. He had brought along a collapsible golf club—a six iron, to be specific. He thought it would be fun to whack golf balls on the moon.

Don't believe me? Look it up. That's why they invented the internet.

"Alan Shepard was the first and only interplanetary golfer," Coke told his sister.

"He was also the first and only interplanetary *litterbug*," Moe said. "What he did was disgraceful."

"It was just a couple of golf balls," Coke told Moe. "What's the big deal?"

"Do you think the universe is your toobleshmoot? Your garbage can?" asked Moe.

"Hey, don't look at *me*," Coke said. "I didn't litter on the moon."

"Wait a minute," Pep interrupted. "Are you saying that you came all the way here to pick up a couple of golf balls that Alan Shepard left on the moon back in 1971?"

"No," Moe told her. "I am saying that we came all the way here for *you two* to pick up the golf balls that Alan Shepard left on the moon back in 1971."

"You gotta be kidding me," Coke said, laughing.

"Sweegling in space is a serious offense!" Moe said. "I mean, littering."

"But we'll *die* if we go out there!" Pep said, clinging to her brother.

That was certainly true. Aside from the fact that there's no air to breathe on the moon, the temperature during the day can reach 250 degrees. At night, it gets down to 290 degrees below zero. Nobody could survive that.

Curly and Larry came into the room with two bulky suits and helmets, not unlike the ones the Apollo astronauts had worn.

"Put these on," Moe instructed the twins. "They will regulate your temperature and supply oxygen so you can breathe."

"And if we refuse?" Coke said.

"We throw you out there *without* the suits, and you die instantly," Moe said matter-of-factly. "It is entirely your choice."

The twins put on the suits.

As she pulled the helmet over her head, Pep was reminded of the day this whole crazy adventure had started. It was high on the cliffs just north of San Francisco. She and Coke had been walking home from school when they'd realized they were being followed by those bowler dudes in golf carts. A woman named Mya had come out of nowhere and given each of them a wingsuit to put on. They'd resisted at first, until a bowler dude had pulled out a blowgun and shot Mya in the neck with a poisoned dart. The twins had put on the wingsuits and jumped off the cliff. The suits saved their lives. Hopefully, these new suits would do it again.

"Okay," said Moe. "Into the decompression chamber."

The twins were led to a sealed room that separated the inside of the ship from the outside.

"Do you think we're going to die out there?" Pep asked. Coke heard her speak through a speaker system in his helmet.

"We'll know soon enough," he replied, trying to

hide his nervousness.

"Open the exterior exit," said Moe's voice.

A door slid open in front of them. Instinctively, the twins took a deep breath of air, as if it would be their last. It wasn't. They could breathe normally. They were looking out on the moon. In the distance, they could see rocks as big as houses.

"Be careful," Moe's voice spoke in their helmets. "You will not be weightless, but you will weigh a lot less than you did on Earth. An object that weighs 100 pounds on your planet weighs about 17 pounds on the moon."

Coke turned around so he could climb down the ladder backward. There were seven steps. He took them one at a time, very slowly and tentatively. After the last step, he lowered his right foot to the surface of the moon.

"That's one small step for a kid—" he started to say.

"Oh, shut up!" Pep shouted. "Let's just find the stupid golf balls and get *out* of here!"

Coke put his other foot on the surface and stepped aside so his sister could follow him down the ladder.

"Can you believe this?" Coke gushed. "We're on the moon! You're the first female on the freaking *moon*!"

"Retrieve the golf balls, please," Moe's voice said in Coke's helmet.

It took a few minutes for Coke and Pep to get used to walking on the moon. The surface, they discovered, was a fine dust, sort of like the ash that's left over after charcoal briquettes have burned out. Their boots left footprints whenever they were lifted up.

"Going to hunt for golf balls," Coke said.

Pep followed as he bounded away from the ship, taking increasingly larger hops as he became more comfortable in lunar gravity. There was no concern about wind or bad weather, because there was no air. There was also no sound. Sound needs air to travel. All the twins could hear was the sound inside their helmets.

"You know what I don't like about this place?" Coke asked as they hopped around searching for golf balls.

"What?" his sister asked.

"It has no atmosphere," he replied, and then erupted into cackling laughter.

"I can't believe you're cracking jokes," Pep said. "Did it occur to you that all these craters were caused by meteorites? How do we know another one isn't going to come down any second and flatten us?"

"Because the last big meteorite shower took place three billion years ago," Coke told her. "So you can relax."

Pep stopped for a moment to look up at the sky. It

was pitch-black, of course, and millions of stars from other galaxies were shining brightly. The earth sat on one side of the horizon, the sun on the other. Up until that moment, it had never occurred to her that the moon and the sun appeared to be about the same size in the sky. In fact, that's only because the sun is four hundred times farther away than the moon. The sun is *huge*, and the moon is only 2,160 miles across— shorter than the drive they took cross-country.

"I found one!" Coke suddenly shouted.

Pep rushed over to see the golf ball, halfway buried in moon dust. Coke picked it up, being careful not to topple over in the bulky suit. A few minutes later, Pep found the other golf ball about thirty yards away. She gave it to her brother to hold.

"Okay, let's get out of here before we run out of air," Pep said.

They hopped and bounded back to the ship, taking time to stop and kick up a little moon dust along the way. When he reached the bottom of the ladder, Coke stepped aside so his sister could climb up first. He took one more long look around at the surface of the moon. This was something he wanted to remember for the rest of his life. Then he followed Pep back up the ladder and into the spaceship.

The exterior door slid shut behind them automatically. A few seconds later the door in front of them opened. Moe, Larry, and Curly were standing there.

"Here are the dumb golf balls," Coke said, handing them over. "On behalf of Alan Shepard and all Earthlings, we apologize for littering."

"Apology accepted," Moe said. "See that you don't do it again."

I know what you're thinking, dear reader. You're thinking that this story is *totally* preposterous. There's no way Coke and Pep could have been abducted by aliens and taken to the moon to retrieve Alan Shepard's golf balls. That simply could never happen in real life.

Well, let me tell you something. If you had lived back in the 18th century and somebody told you there would eventually be cars and telephones and radio and TV and motion pictures, you would have said it was totally preposterous.

If you had lived in the 19th century and somebody told you there would eventually be airplanes and personal computers and video games and satellites, you would have said it was totally preposterous.

Even at the end of the 20th century, when your parents were children, if somebody had told them that eventually there would be the internet and pocket-size telephones that could access virtually all the world's information in seconds, they would have said it was totally preposterous.

And yet, all those totally preposterous things happened. So who's to say it's preposterous for beings from another planet to come visit us on Earth and take us for a ride to the moon to retrieve Alan Shepard's golf balls?

Amazing things are going to happen in the 21st century, too, and the best part is that you're going to be lucky enough to witness them.

Safely back inside the ship, Coke and Pep removed the spacesuits that had kept them alive on the surface of the moon. The ship blasted off smoothly once again, and the ride back to Earth was uneventful. The twins were still so excited about what they had seen and done, the time went by quickly.

Soon the blue marble with white swirls that is planet Earth was visible. Home sweet home.

It was evening. As the ship got closer to the ground, Coke and Pep could see lights out the window. It was unclear where they were landing. For all they knew, they were in a different city, or a different country.

But at least they were home, on their own planet. That was the important thing. They could always find their way back to their parents somehow.

The ship touched down with a slight bump, and the door opened once again. Moe, Larry, and Curly walked the twins to the exit. With all they had been through, Coke and Pep expected that there might be some kind of a formal farewell. They figured that the aliens might even extend a hand of friendship or (ugh) want to give them a hug.

But none of that happened.

"You may go," Moe said unceremoniously. "And remember, no sweegling. I mean, littering."

Chapter 9
HOME SWEET HOME

"**L**et's blow this pop stand!" Coke shouted as he and Pep scrambled down the ladder of the spaceship, jumping off the last few steps and tumbling to the grass. Pep got on her hands and knees and kissed the ground. It felt so good to be home.

"I can't believe we made it back," Pep said, giggling uncontrollably. "I thought it was all over for us."

Seconds later, the spaceship lifted off, kicking up a swirl of dust in the air. The twins shielded their faces and watched as the ship took off and disappeared as quietly as it had arrived. In seconds, it was gone.

"Wow," Coke said. "Did that really happen, or did I just have some weird alien abduction dream?"

"If that was a dream," his sister replied, "I had it, too."

It was nighttime. A half-moon hung in the sky. As they looked up, it was hard for the twins to believe that they had been standing on that surface, and now they were standing on Earth.

There were trees on all sides. There was no obvious path leading back to civilization.

"Where are we?" Pep asked.

"I have no clue," Coke replied. "This could be anywhere."

"I hope we're at least in the United States," Pep said. "We don't have any money or identification or anything. They won't let us on a flight home."

"Come on," Coke told her, holding out his hand. "Follow me. I think this is the way."

They walked through the woods, Coke holding his arms up in front of him to push aside the branches and bushes. He had a good sense of direction and seemed instinctively to know which way to go. At one point, the thorns on a bush caught on the sleeve of his T-shirt and tore it.

"I'm scared," Pep said. "It's dark."

"You just survived an alien abduction," Coke

reminded her as he stepped over a fallen branch. "You survived a trip to the moon. You can handle a little darkness."

Through the trees, it appeared that there was a light in the distance. Coke headed in that direction, confident of his navigation skills.

"How much time do you think has passed since we were . . . uh, kidnapped?" Pep asked, still holding her brother's hand.

"Can't say for sure," Coke replied. "I mean, we flew 239,000 miles to the *moon*, then back. It didn't feel like a long time, but maybe time moves faster in outer space. Didn't Einstein prove that? It could have been a few days. It could have been a few weeks, for all I know."

"If we were gone that long, there was probably a big manhunt for us," Pep said. "Hey, I bet we made the local news."

"Local news? Are you kidding?" her brother said. "We made the *national* news. And when they find out we're alive, we're going to be the most famous kids on the *planet*."

"You really think so?" Pep asked.

"We were abducted by aliens!" Coke told her. "We walked on the *moon*! We picked up Alan Shepard's golf balls! This is going to blow everybody's *minds* when they find out. We could make a million dollars selling our story to the tabloids. I may have to get a publicist to fend off all the requests for interviews."

Pep pondered her potential celebrity as they made their way through the woods. She had mixed feelings about the whole thing. It could be cool to be a little famous. But she didn't want to be pestered by paparazzi or have everything she did reported in the tabloids.

The light in the distance was closer now. It looked like a neon sign. The twins couldn't make out the letters yet.

"Do you think there will be TV cameras?" Pep asked her brother. "How does my hair look? If we're going to be on TV, I want to look good."

"You look fine," Coke said dismissively.

Soon, they came to a clearing at the edge of the woods. They could see the back of a building.

"Look!" Coke said, pointing at the ping-pong table where they had been playing when the spaceship arrived.

"They brought us back to the exact same spot!" Pep shouted. "I can't wait to see the looks on Mom and Dad's faces when they see us."

"I'm sure Mom and Dad aren't here anymore," Coke replied. "They're probably back home in California by now."

The twins passed the ping-pong table and walked around to the front of the motel. There was a man at the ice machine scooping ice cubes into a plastic bucket. When he turned around, they could tell it was their father.

"I thought you kids went to bed," Dr. McDonald said matter-of-factly. "It's late. What are you still doing up?"

"Dad!" Coke and Pep shouted, wrapping their arms around him tightly. "We love you so much!"

Dr. McDonald was taken aback by this sudden show of affection from his children, but he wasn't about to complain. The emotions displayed by teenagers always seem to be on a roller coaster.

"I'll never do a bad thing ever again," Pep said, refusing to let go of her father. "I'll never complain or criticize you or roll my eyes when you say something stupid."

"Uh, okay. Good," said Dr. McDonald.

"Where's the media?" asked Coke. "Did the camera crews go home? I want to make a statement to the press."

"Camera crews? Media? Press?" asked Dr. McDonald. "What are you talking about?"

"Didn't the police come?" asked Coke. "Didn't you file a missing persons report on us?"

"Missing persons report?" said Dr. McDonald. "You said you were going to play a little ping-pong a couple of hours ago. I assumed that's what you've been doing."

"A couple of hours ago?" asked Pep.

"We did play ping-pong," Coke explained quickly. "But then we heard a noise and it was an alien spaceship and we went to check it out and we got sucked up into the spaceship and then it took off and the aliens were really ugly and we went to the moon and they made us pick up Alan Shepard's golf balls and then they brought us back. And here we are!"

Dr. McDonald looked at Coke for a moment. Then he burst out laughing.

"How do you come *up* with this stuff?" he asked, doubling over. "I *wish* I had such a vivid imagination!"

At that moment, one of the motel room doors opened and Mrs. McDonald came out.

"Ben, where's that ice you went to get?" she shouted.

"Mommy!" the twins hollered, running over to her. "We love you!"

Mrs. McDonald looked at her husband quizzically as Coke and Pep wrapped their arms around her. He just rolled his eyes and said one word—"Kids!"

"What happened to your shirt?" Mrs. McDonald asked Coke, poking her finger through the hole. "How do you rip a shirt playing *ping-pong*? Why can't you keep your clothes nice for a change? These things are expensive, you know."

"He must have ripped it while he was picking up golf balls from the moon," said Dr. McDonald with a snort.

"What are you talking about, Ben?" asked Mrs. McDonald.

"I'll tell you later," Dr. McDonald said. "Let's get to sleep, everybody. We have a big day ahead of us. It's a long drive back to California."

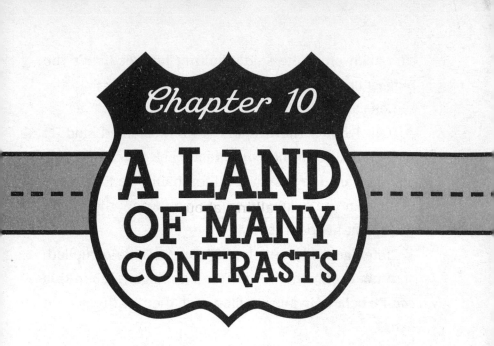

Chapter 10

A LAND OF MANY CONTRASTS

"Are we there yet?" Coke hollered from the backseat.

Dr. McDonald laughed. He had just pulled the Ferrari 612 Scaglietti out of the parking lot of the Best Western El Rancho Palacio in Roswell, New Mexico.

"Very funny," he replied.

Leaving Roswell, he drove past the International UFO Museum and Research Center, the Alien Zone, and a bunch of alien-themed gift shops.

"I can't believe how many people actually fall for

this alien crap," he said, shaking his head. "It's the biggest con job I've ever seen."

Coke and Pep shot looks at each other.

"Oh, I don't know, dear," Mrs. McDonald said. "I saw an article in the paper last week that said there could be as many as forty billion habitable Earth-size planets in the galaxy. How do you know there isn't intelligent life out there?"

"Intelligent life out there?" Dr. McDonald replied. "I'm not even convinced there's intelligent life in this *car*. I'll believe in aliens when I see them with my own eyes."

"I'm with you, Dad," Coke said, winking at his sister. "What a con job."

The twins shared a secret laugh. There was no point trying to convince their parents that just a few hours earlier they had been walking on the moon and searching for Alan Shepard's golf balls for some uptight aliens who had a thing about littering.

The *nice* thing was that their brief adventure in outer space had completely knocked Coke and Pep's *other* problems out of their minds. They had just about forgotten about the evil Dr. Herman Warsaw, Mrs. Higgins, Doominator, and those nincompoop bowler dudes who had been chasing them across the United States for the last four weeks. It was like a man with a stomachache who accidentally smashes his thumb with a hammer. Suddenly, he's not thinking about his stomachache anymore.

"Go West, young man!" Dr. McDonald bellowed as he pulled the Ferrari onto Route 70, the major road out of Roswell. The engine purred to life as he pushed his foot against the accelerator.

"How many miles is it to San Francisco?" Pep asked.

Mrs. McDonald had her laptop computer open in the front seat. She tapped a few keys and reported that they had about 1,300 miles ahead of them, depending on which route they took to California.

"If we drove straight without making any stops," Mrs. McDonald said, "we would be home in less than twenty hours."

If you'd like to follow the McDonalds on their trip back to California, it's easy. Get on the internet and go to Google Maps (http://maps.google.com/), Mapquest (www.mapquest.com), Rand McNally (www.randmcnally.com) or whatever navigation website you like best.

On Google Maps, click Get Directions. In the A box, type Roswell NM. In the B box, type Alamogordo NM. Then click Get Directions again.

See the map? It would be a straight shot on Route 70 that morning for more than a hundred miles.

Twenty hours. Both of the twins thought the same thing—soon, their nightmare would be over.

Mrs. McDonald took out her New Mexico guidebook. The southern part of the state is mostly desert and boiling hot in the summer months.

"It says here that New Mexico is a land of many contrasts," she reported. "Sun-baked deserts, deep caves, and snow-covered mountains. Big, modern cities and thousand-year-old Indian villages. Did you know that in the Aztec language, the word *Mexico* means 'in the center of the moon'?"

"Actually, I *did* know that," Coke said, looking out the window.

His sister rolled her eyes, knowing that her brother wasn't just boasting. He *did* know just about everything. That's what happens when you're born with a photographic memory.

"Hey, there's a museum devoted to Billy the Kid in Fort Sumner," Mrs. McDonald said excitedly. "And in Faywood, New Mexico, there's a rock formation that looks just like a giant toilet."

Both sites would be perfect to gather material for her popular website, *Amazing but True*. Unfortunately (or perhaps fortunately, depending on your point of view), it would be necessary to drive hundreds of miles out of the way to visit them.

"Personally," Dr. McDonald said, "I would be more interested in learning about New Mexico's involvement in the space program and the birth of the atomic bomb."

"Bo-ring!" both kids hooted.

"Dad, you are such a stick-in-the-mud," Pep said.

"I vote for the big toilet," said Coke.

"Big toilet! Big toilet! Big toilet!" the twins chanted.

"Knock it off back there!" shouted Dr. McDonald.

When we think of the desert, a lot of people think of the Sahara in Africa—smooth, desolate, rolling sand dunes sculpted by the wind. But the desert of the American southwest doesn't look anything like that. It's mostly flat with low shrubs, interrupted by occasional road signs. There wasn't much to look at out the window.

The twins read or listened to music while Mrs. McDonald—as usual—spent the time planning their route and looking up interesting places to visit. She had already decided that today's destination would be Alamogordo, New Mexico. And because the money from *Amazing but True* had paid for the trip, she got to make most of the decisions.

"Hey, look at this," she said after they'd been driving for an hour. "We're not that far from Smokey Bear Museum."

"*Please* tell me that we don't have to go there, Mom," Pep begged. "It sounds lame."

"You don't know *anything* about Smokey Bear Museum," her mother admonished. "You shouldn't criticize what you don't know."

"I know it's a museum about a cartoon bear," Pep said.

"Shouldn't that be Smokey *the* Bear?" asked Dr. McDonald.

"No, his official name is Smokey Bear," replied Mrs. McDonald. "That's what it says in the guidebook."

"Maybe *the* is Smokey's middle name," suggested Coke.

In any case, Mrs. McDonald decided to bypass Smokey Bear Museum. She had other ideas. At Tularosa, Route 70 bends south. Just a few miles from Alamogordo, they saw this in the distance. . . .

"What the heck is *that*?" asked Dr. McDonald.

"It looks like a big pistachio nut," Pep said.

"It *is* a big pistachio nut," said Coke.

"Not only is it a big pistachio nut," reported Mrs. McDonald gleefully, "it's the biggest pistachio nut in the *world*!"

"Here we go again," groaned Dr. McDonald, slapping his forehead. He stepped on the gas, hoping that if the car was moving fast enough, maybe he wouldn't be asked to stop.

"Oh, come on, Ben!" Mrs. McDonald said. "It's right off the road here. How could we go to Alamogordo, New Mexico, and *not* visit the world's largest pistachio nut?"

"Yeah, lighten up, Dad," said Coke.

Dr. McDonald rolled his eyes and stamped on the brake. As a distinguished history professor at San Francisco State University, he had little regard for the tacky roadside attractions his wife and children found so fascinating. It was one of the few things they argued about.

"I need to use the bathroom anyway," he said, skidding off the highway just before he would have passed the giant pistachio.

"Cool!" the twins shouted as they hopped out of the car and ran over for a close-up view.

At thirty feet tall, and covered with thirty-five gallons of paint, the giant pistachio sculpture was undeniably cool. Its tan shell was partly open, and the nut inside had been painted bright green.

"You don't see one of *these* every day," Mrs. McDonald said as she snapped photos and took notes for *Amazing but True*. The twins debated whether or not the pistachio was bigger than the world's largest frying pan or the world's largest yo-yo, both of which they had seen earlier in the trip.

As it turned out, the giant pistachio is the calling card for the McGuinn Pistachio Tree Ranch, a working farm with 12,500 trees and 6,000 wine-producing grapevines. It has become an institution in the Alamogordo area.

A few minutes later, Dr. McDonald found the rest of the family in the McGuinn gift shop, examining the dizzying selection of pistachio-themed treats and knickknacks.

"It's a tourist trap," he grumbled. "They just want you to buy their stuff."

"We know," Pep said, offering him a bite of Atomic Hot Chili Pistachio Brittle. "We did."

The town of Alamogordo sits at the base of the Sacramento Mountains; its name means "fat cottonwood tree" in Spanish. The smell of roasted nuts triggered hunger pangs, so the McDonalds got back on the four-lane road and drove a mile toward town to the first restaurant they saw, the Rustic Café. The Rustic Café's claim to fame is a sixteen-ounce hamburger. If you're counting, that's a *pound* of meat. Anyone who can eat the whole thing gets a T-shirt and their picture up on the wall. None of the McDonalds attempted such a feat.

After lunch, Mrs. McDonald instructed her husband to turn left on Scenic Drive for three miles, then another quick left up a hill. Soon they came to a huge modern glass building with a rocket ship mounted in front of it. A sign read . . .

New Mexico Museum of Space History

"Now, *this* is more like it," Dr. McDonald said as he found a parking spot. "Maybe you kids will actually *learn* something here."

"Not another museum!" Coke whined.

"Oh, I didn't bring us here for the museum," Mrs. McDonald said as she got out of the car. "I brought us here to pay our respects."

"Pay our respects? To whom?" asked Pep.

The family walked to the front of the museum. On the grass near the flagpole, they found this. . . .

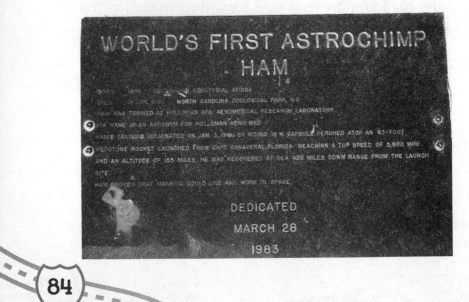

WORLD'S FIRST ASTROCHIMP
HAM

BORN 1955 IN EQUATORIAL AFRICA
DIED 19 JAN. 1983 NORTH CAROLINA ZOOLOGICAL PARK, N.C.
HAM WAS TRAINED AT HOLLOMAN AFB, AEROMEDICAL RESEARCH LABORATORY.
THE NAME IS AN ACRONYM FOR HOLLOMAN AERO MED.
HAM'S TRAINING CULMINATED ON JAN. 3, 1961, BY RIDING IN A CAPSULE PERCHED ATOP AN 83-FOOT
REDSTONE ROCKET LAUNCHED FROM CAPE CANAVERAL, FLORIDA, REACHING A TOP SPEED OF 5,900 MPH
AND AN ALTITUDE OF 155 MILES. HE WAS RECOVERED AT SEA 420 MILES DOWN RANGE FROM THE LAUNCH
SITE.
HAM PROVED THAT MANKIND COULD LIVE AND WORK IN SPACE.

DEDICATED
MARCH 28
1983

"You gotta be kidding me," Coke said. "A monkey grave?"

Not just *any* monkey. Before NASA was willing to risk human lives in the space program, they sent animals. Ham the Astrochimp was the first American in outer space.

A few other families came over to look at the gravesite. Mrs. McDonald pulled out her camera.

Ham blasted off from Cape Canaveral in January of 1961. He traveled 155 miles in 16.5 minutes and splashed down safely in the Atlantic Ocean. Three months later, Alan Shepard (the astronaut/golfer) became America's first *human* astronaut.

"I wonder what happened to Ham after his flight," Pep said.

"He retired," a guy looking at the plaque explained. "He lived at the National Zoo in Washington for seventeen years. Then he died in 1983 at age twenty-seven."

"Let us have a moment of silence in honor of Ham the Astrochimp," suggested Mrs. McDonald.

"Are you sure it shouldn't be Ham Astrochimp?" Pep asked. "Like Smokey Bear?"

"I guess in this case Ham's middle name really was *the*," said Coke.

After paying his respects to "the flying monkey"

(as Coke put it), Dr. McDonald wasn't about to leave. He insisted that the whole family go inside the museum, and they were glad they did. The New Mexico Museum of Space History was full of displays that everyone in the family enjoyed: Robert Goddard's early rocket experiments near Roswell. A mock-up of the International Space Station. A moon rock. A space toilet. A memorial garden tribute to astronauts who had died. The International Space Hall of Fame. Even Coke learned a few things he didn't already know.

By the time the McDonalds had seen everything there was to see in the museum, it was getting late. They stopped off at a fast food drive-through window for dinner and drove down White Sands Boulevard to the White Sands Motel to sleep for the night.

All in all, it had been a good day. To the twins, of course, *any* day in which they hadn't been attacked, set on fire, lowered into boiling oil, frozen, kidnapped by aliens, or thrown off a cliff was a good day. Their tormentors—Dr. Warsaw, Evil

Go to Google Maps (http://maps.google.com).

Click Get Directions.

In the A box, type Alamogordo NM.

In the B box, type Socorro NM.

Click Get Directions.

Elvis, Doominator, Mrs. Higgins, and the bowler dudes—seemed to be a million miles away.

"Maybe they forgot about us," Pep said as she turned off the light for the night. "Maybe they'll leave us alone from now on."

Or maybe not.

Chapter 11

GROUND ZERO

At this point, you're probably starting to feel a little angry that Coke hasn't been thrown into a volcano yet. I mean, I promised back in chapter 1 that Coke was going to get thrown into a volcano. And here we are in chapter 11, and the twins are nowhere *near* a volcano. Do they even *have* volcanoes in New Mexico?

Again, I ask you to show a little patience. Trust me, by the end of this story Coke will get thrown into a volcano. You can take that to the bank.

Dr. McDonald put the Ferrari in gear and headed

north out of Alamogordo on Route 54. Coke already had his earbuds in and was nodding his head, oblivious to the world around him.

"Where are we going today?" Pep asked from the backseat.

"We'll tell you when we get there," her father replied.

"Is it a surprise?"

"Let's just say we're going someplace that *everyone* should see," he said.

"I love a mystery," Pep said, rubbing her hands together.

"It's not that kind of mystery," said Mrs. McDonald mysteriously.

The two-lane road cut through the New Mexico desert on a straight line for mile after mile. The most interesting thing to look at was the occasional SPEED LIMIT 55 sign at the side of the road. Pep dozed off for a while, waking up in time to see her mother telling Dr. McDonald to slow down and turn left onto an unmarked road.

RESTRICTED USAGE ROAD, a small sign said.

About two hours after they had left Alamogordo, another sign appeared, announcing that they were approaching WHITE SANDS MISSILE RANGE. Dr. McDonald continued down the road for a few miles until he came to yet *another* sign. He stopped the car and instructed everyone to get out. Coke turned off his music.

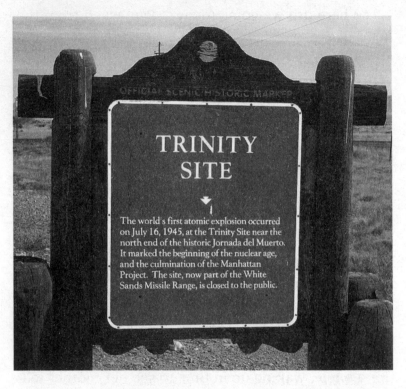

"This is the Trinity Site," Dr. McDonald said solemnly. "After years of working on an atomic bomb, this is where we dropped it. Nobody knew if the thing was going to explode, because it was the first time they had ever tested it. But it did. It blew up with the force of eighteen kilotons of TNT. Two hundred miles away, windows were rattling."

"Wow," Coke said, not just pretending to be impressed, but genuinely impressed. "And it happened right here?"

"Not *exactly* here," his father said. "It was a few miles down the road."

"Can we go to the actual site?" Pep asked.

"It's still radioactive," her father replied. "Seventy years later, and it's still radioactive. But I wanted you kids to know about this. It was the birth of the atomic age. A few weeks later, we dropped the bomb on Hiroshima, and you know what happened there."

"Eighty thousand people died right away," Coke said, remembering an article he'd read, "and something like a hundred and forty thousand died later, from radiation."

Mrs. McDonald took a photo of the sign for *Amazing but True*. She opened her guidebook and read a quote from Robert Oppenheimer, the mastermind behind the first atomic bomb: "'Now I am become Death, the destroyer of worlds.'"

For a few minutes, none of the McDonalds said anything. There were no snarky jokes or wisecracks from the twins. It didn't seem like the time or place.

"Why did we do it?" Pep finally asked. "Why did we build such a horrible thing?"

"It was during World War Two," Dr. McDonald told

her. "If we hadn't built an atomic bomb, Hitler would have built one."

"You can imagine what would have happened if he did it first," said Mrs. McDonald.

"I always wanted to come here," Dr. McDonald said, "and I wanted you kids to come here too. Hopefully, in your lifetime, nobody will *ever* use an atomic weapon again. Okay, let's go."

Back on the road, it was obvious why this part of New Mexico had been chosen for the first nuclear test. There was *nothing* around as far as the eye could see. Or maybe it was the opposite—there was nothing around because there had been a nuclear test here. Nobody wanted to get radiation poisoning.

In any case, it was a good thing they started the day with a full tank of gas. There was no place to fill up.

Everyone seemed lost in their thoughts when Dr. McDonald suddenly announced, "I think I've got it!"

"What, Ben?" asked Mrs. McDonald.

"This could be my book! I could write a novel about the Trinity Site!"

The others had almost forgotten about Dr. McDonald's recent interest in writing a novel. As a university professor, he had written several nonfiction books in his field of technology. But they were only read by the academic community and had not sold many copies. He wanted to write something that would find a wide audience. He yearned to see his name on the best-seller list.

"What *about* the Trinity Site, Dad?" Pep asked.

"Maybe I could write about a family like ours that was on vacation in 1945," Dr. McDonald suggested. "What if they were driving through New Mexico at the moment the first atomic bomb detonated? What would happen to them? How would it change their lives? That might make an interesting story."

"They would have been incinerated," Coke said.

"That would depend on how many miles they were from ground zero," said his mother.

"Hey, there's my title," Dr. McDonald said. "*Ground Zero.*"

The family continued brainstorming ideas about Dr. McDonald's novel, which helped make the end-less New Mexico miles seem to roll by just a little more quickly. After an hour, they stopped for lunch in the town of Socorro at a Mexican place called Armijo's.

At that point, the plan was to continue up the high-way eighty miles to Albuquerque. But after looking through her New Mexico guidebook, Mrs. McDonald said to turn onto a smaller road—Route 60 West.

"It will be less than an hour, Ben," she promised. "It will be worth it."

Dr. McDonald wiped the sweat off his forehead with a handkerchief and reluctantly pulled off the highway, as his wife suggested. After all, he reminded himself, it was the money from *Amazing but True* that had paid for the trip.

It certainly didn't *seem* like the detour would be worth it. More desert. More heat. More nothing. A sign announced the approach of Cibola National Forest, but Mrs. McDonald had another destination in mind.

"Turn here, Ben," she said at a sign that simply said 52.

Off in the distance to the right, dozens of white structures came into view, evenly spaced apart. They didn't look like buildings.

A few miles closer, the structures could be seen more clearly. They looked sort of like orange squeezers, or maybe giant ray guns pointed at the sky.

Closer still, and it was clear what they really were—satellite dishes. And they were *enormous*. From up close, it was an awe-inspiring sight.

"What *is* this place, Mom?" Pep asked, staring out the window.

"These are the most powerful radio telescopes in the world," her mother said, reading from her

guidebook. "Astronomers from all over converge on this spot in New Mexico to scan deep space for sound waves and signals that come from billions of light-years away."

At that moment, the giant dish they were looking at began to rotate slowly, swiveling around to the right.

"Cool!" the twins said.

Dr. McDonald parked at the Karl G. Jansky Very Large Array Visitor Center. Yes, that's what it's called. An "array," according to Mrs. McDonald's guidebook, is a series of telescopes that work together.

A pleasant lady behind the front desk told them there were twenty-seven radio antennas altogether, each one eighty-two feet in diameter and weighing 230 tons.

"Put together, they're as powerful as one regular telescope . . . if that telescope was twenty-two miles in diameter."

"Wow," Pep said.

"Any questions?" the lady asked.

"Do those things pick up HBO?" Coke asked, snickering.

The lady chuckled, the laugh of someone who's heard a joke a thousand times but doesn't want to hurt the joke-teller's feelings.

"No," she said, "but they do receive electromagnetic emissions of quasars, pulsars, supernovas, gamma rays, black holes, signals from satellites, things like that. And despite what you may have heard, they are *not* used to search for aliens."

"But if there *were* aliens out there," Dr. McDonald said, "this would be a great way for them to communicate with us, right?"

"I suppose so, yes," the lady replied.

Coke looked at his sister.

"Or, they could just land their spaceship in the back of a motel," he muttered.

The lady suggested the family visit the small museum in the next room and watch a short film about radio astronomy. There was no formal tour, she explained, but visitors were allowed to take a self-guided walk around the satellite dishes.

"It's a bit too hot out there for me," Dr. McDonald said, wiping his brow again. "I'll check out the museum."

"I'll be with Dad," said Mrs. McDonald. "You kids can take the walking tour if you'd like."

As the twins stepped outside, they saw this sign . . .

WALKING TOUR
CAUTION
WATCH OUT
FOR SNAKES

"I don't like snakes," Coke said, carefully scanning the ground in front of him as the twins tiptoed over to the first stop on the tour. It was labeled WHISPER GALLERY, and it consisted 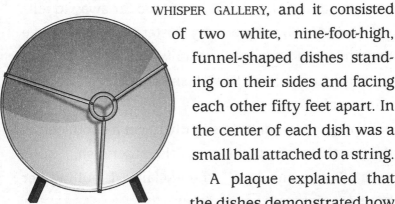 of two white, nine-foot-high, funnel-shaped dishes standing on their sides and facing each other fifty feet apart. In the center of each dish was a small ball attached to a string.

A plaque explained that the dishes demonstrated how sound waves can be gathered and amplified. When you whisper into the center of one dish, the sound bounces off the dish and directly to the other one, fifty feet away. So two people can whisper to each other even though they're not next to one another.

"Go stand at the other dish," Coke told his sister. "Let's try it out."

"Two other people are already over there," Pep replied.

Coke stuck his face close to the center of the dish.

Suddenly, a male voice whispered, "Don't turn around."

"What? Who said that?" Pep asked.

"Shhhh!" the voice said. "Quiet, Pep! I said don't turn around."

The twins turned around anyway to see who was standing at the other dish. It was too far away to tell.

"How do you know my sister's name?" Coke demanded, in a whisper. "Who *is* this?"

"Who do you *think* it is?" asked another voice, this one female.

Pep squinted her eyes slightly to get a good look at the people standing in front of the other dish.

"It's Bones and Mya!" she exclaimed, pulling her brother's sleeve. "They're *here*!"

Now, if you've been following the Genius Files, you know who Bones and Mya are. They were the ones who recruited the twins into The Genius Files program in the first place, and they had been lifesavers already on more than one occasion.

"Shhhh!" Mya whispered. "It's important that you stay quiet. No one can hear us. We must not be seen together."

"What is it?" Pep asked, whispering into the dish.

"I'm afraid we have some bad news," Bones said.

"We can take it," Coke whispered.

"We've picked up some chatter," said Mya. "According to our sources, Dr. Warsaw is attempting to build a nuclear weapon."

"No!" said Pep, taking an involuntary step back.

"Are you kidding me?" asked Coke.

"Nuclear weapons are something we *never* kid about," said Bones. "This is for real."

"The old guy must have truly gone off the deep end," said Pep. "But why would he want a nuke? What's the logic?"

"Logic doesn't apply to people like Dr. Warsaw," Mya replied. "We can't explain why insane people do the things they do. Sometimes they just want attention. Sometimes they want to threaten you, or blackmail you. And sometimes, they're just crazy enough to harm other people or themselves. We have to expect that's a possibility, and prepare for it."

"Do you mean Dr. Warsaw might set off an atomic bomb?" Coke asked. "Like the one that was dropped on Hiroshima?"

"Yes, but much more powerful," said Bones, "and much smaller. These days, it's possible to build a bomb that would fit inside a briefcase."

"He is apparently trying to accumulate enough nuclear material to make one dirty bomb," Mya added. "We fear he will set it off."

"When?" Pep asked.

"We don't know precisely," Mya whispered back. "Soon. Possibly in the next few weeks. Probably in a public place so it will do the most damage."

"Where?" Pep asked.

"We don't know."

"How?" Pep asked.

"We don't know that, either."

"You don't know a whole lot, do you?" Coke said, annoyed.

"We know that we've got to stop him," Bones replied.

"And where do *we* fit into all this?" Coke asked. "In case you didn't notice, we're *thirteen*. We didn't sign up to save the world."

"No, but the two of you are very mature, and quite capable," Mya said. "You've proven that time and time again."

"Don't you think we've done *enough*?" asked Pep. "Why don't you ask somebody *else* to save the world? There are plenty of kids in The Genius Files program. Why can't one of *them* stop Dr. Warsaw?"

"Yeah, we want out," Coke added. "We just want to get back to California and live our normal lives again."

"It's too late for that, I'm sorry to say," Bones told them. "You have a relationship with Dr. Warsaw. Your aunt was even *married* to him before she died. You're *related*. You're involved. We *need* you."

"The fate of the world may depend on this," said Mya.

Coke and Pep looked at each other, communicating silently. *How did we get sucked into this? What would happen if Dr. Warsaw was able to set off a nuclear bomb? When does it all end?*

"You're certainly not giving us much to go on," Pep whispered.

"We're working on that," said Bones. "A *lot* of people are working on it, believe me. I *do* have one piece of information to give you. I don't know if this might be helpful. It seems to be some kind of code. The letters don't mean anything to us. It may mean something to you . . ."

Bones took a piece of paper out of his pocket and read it—letter by letter—to the twins . . .

NEZVES YZTRIH TNEETEN ZINHTH GIEYTZ NEWZTYAM

"Got it," Coke said.

"Don't you need to write those letters down?" asked Mya.

"He memorized it," Pep said. "He has a photographic memory. He remembers *everything.*"

Pep turned around to see if Bones and Mya had a reaction to that. But they were gone.

Before we close this chapter, dear reader, I know what you're thinking—*Where are the snakes?*

Any time you're reading a story or watching a movie and the characters are warned about something, that very thing is *sure* to threaten them later on.

It was the great Russian author Chekhov who wrote, "If you say in the first chapter that there is a rifle hanging on the wall, in the second or third chapter it absolutely must go off. If it's not going to be fired, it shouldn't be hanging there."

You've probably noticed that if a character in a movie coughs, later on they're sure to get lung cancer or some other horrible disease. Nobody coughs in a movie just because they have a tickle in their throat.

These are common devices used in storytelling.

When Coke and Pep walked by the sign warning them to watch for snakes, you probably figured it was only a matter of time before they were attacked by snakes.

Please, reader, don't assume *anything*. You know what they say—to ASSUME is to make an ASS of U and ME.

Trust me. There are no snakes.

Chapter 12
THE FIRST CIPHER

"**H**ow was the tour of the satellite dishes?" their
father asked when the twins got back to the
visitor center.

"Bo-ring."

"Bo-ring," of course, was Coke and Pep's default
reply whenever their parents asked them about
anything. They didn't mention anything about the
meeting with Mya and Bones.

Once they were back in the car, Mrs. McDonald
gave each twin a souvenir she had purchased in the
gift shop—a package of freeze-dried ice cream like

the kind astronauts eat. Coke stuffed the package in his pocket. Pep opened hers right away and munched it as she copied down the cipher that Bones and Mya had delivered, in neat handwriting on a clean page of her notepad.

NEZVES YZTRIH TNEETEN ZINHTH GIEYTZ NEWZTYAM

What could *that* possibly mean?

Dr. McDonald retraced his steps back to the town of Socorro and then turned north on I-25 toward Albuquerque, the largest city in New Mexico. Of course, that isn't saying much, considering that the entire state only has about two million people living in it. As a comparison, more than *thirty-six million* people live in California.

Worry lines wrinkled Pep's forehead, and she truly had something to worry about. Not only was Dr. Warsaw back on the radar, but now that lunatic was building an atomic briefcase bomb. And he just might be crazy enough to use it.

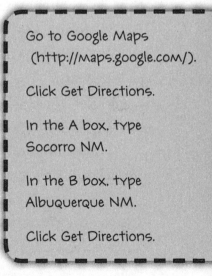

Go to Google Maps (http://maps.google.com/).

Click Get Directions.

In the A box, type Socorro NM.

In the B box, type Albuquerque NM.

Click Get Directions.

Pep got to work. First, she stared at the cipher to see if there were any obvious patterns. . . .

NEZVES YZTRIH TNEETEN ZINHTH
GIEYTZ NEWZTYAM

She copied the letters again, this time closing them up. Spaces between words, she knew, are often put in there just to throw you off.

NEZVESYZTRIHTNEETENZINHTHGIEY
TZNEWZTYAM

"See anything?" Coke whispered, looking over her shoulder.

"Not yet," she whispered back. "NEETEN pops out, but it's probably just some random letters that look like a word."

She copied the cipher once again, this time writing it backward.

MAYTZWENZTYEIGHTHNIZNETEEN
THIRTZYSEVZEN

"Wait a minute!" she said. "I think there are nulls in there."

"You mean fake letters?" Coke asked.

"Yeah, probably Z."

She crossed out all the Zs, and this is what was left . . .

MAYTWENTYEIGHTHNINETEEN
THIRTYSEVEN

"That's *it*!" Coke said, a little too loud. "You're a genius! Add the spaces!"

She didn't have to. It was obvious now.

MAY TWENTY EIGHTH NINETEEN THIRTY SEVEN

"May 28, 1937!" Pep said.

"What do you think *that* could mean?" Coke asked his sister.

"How should I know?" Pep replied. "*You're* the one who remembers everything. Something important must have happened on that date."

"What are you two whispering about back there?" asked Mrs. McDonald.

"Yeah," said their dad. "What mischief are you up to?"

"Oh, we're just playing a word game," Coke told his parents.

"Sounds like fun," said Mrs. McDonald. "Can *we* play, too?"

"No!" said both twins.

The twins looked at each other. They knew they would have to wait a few minutes after being snotty before they could ask a favor of their parents. It was sort of like waiting an hour after you eat before going swimming. Finally, they determined that enough time had passed.

"Hey, *you* guys are old," Coke called up to the front seat. "What does the date May 28, 1937, mean to you?"

"I'm not *that* old," said Dr. McDonald. "Why do you ask?"

"I was just wondering," Coke lied.

"Well, 1937 was shortly before World War Two broke out, if that helps," said Dr. McDonald.

It didn't. Both twins realized that this was too serious for guessing games. Dr. Warsaw was working on a nuclear bomb. From now on, Coke and Pep would have to stop relying on their parents' knowledge to help them figure out these clues. No more fooling around. No more mistakes. Lives could be at stake.

"Google it," Coke said to his sister.

She borrowed her mother's laptop computer and tapped the date into the box. . . .

There were 345,000 results. Pep paged through the

top choices looking for something significant. One thing kept popping up. . . .

MAY 28, 1937: VOLKSWAGEN IS FOUNDED

"That's gotta be it!" Coke whispered. "Volkswagen was Hitler's pet project. I saw that in a book. He wanted a car that average people in Germany could afford to buy. The word *Volkswagen* means 'The People's Car Company.'"

"But what could Volkswagen have to do with *us*?" Pep asked.

"We know Hitler was trying to build an atomic bomb, right?" Coke said. "Well, Dr. Warsaw is trying to build an atomic bomb, too. Maybe they're connected. Maybe Dr. Warsaw is driving a Volkswagen. Maybe we need to go to a Volkswagen factory. Who knows?"

Up to this point, the answers to the ciphers had always led the twins to something *big*. It was never obvious in the beginning, but eventually, all the clues would tie together in some way.

Pep found a clean page in her notepad and wrote this at the top. . . .

CIPHER #1: MAY 28, 1937, VOLKSWAGEN
IS FOUNDED

The twins had been working so hard on the cipher, they hadn't noticed that they were suddenly driving past stores, apartments, and gas stations. They weren't in the desert anymore. Coke looked out the window to see the Albuquerque Plaza Office Tower, the tallest building in New Mexico. It was nice to be in a big city again. Back in civilization.

"So what does the guidebook say about Albuquerque?" Dr. McDonald asked his wife.

"Let's see," she said. "Do you guys want to go to the Turquoise Museum?"

"They have a museum devoted to a *color*?" Pep asked.

"Not a color, you dope," her brother said. "Turquoise is a mineral."

"Don't call your sister a dope," warned Dr. McDonald.

"We already went to the Bauxite Museum," Coke recalled. "I don't want to look at more rocks."

"There's the Meteorite Museum . . ."

"No!"

"How about the International Balloon Museum?" suggested Mrs. McDonald. "Maybe we could take a ride in a hot air balloon."

"I don't like heights," Pep said. "Is there a Volkswagen museum in Albuquerque?"

"No, but there's the American International Rattle-snake Museum."

"Cool!" Pep said. "Let's go there! We learned all about snakes in Girl Scouts. I even got to hold one."

"I don't like snakes," Coke said.

"Come on," his sister urged him. "Don't be such a baby."

🦌

Now reader, I know what you're thinking—somehow, the twins will find themselves confronted by poisonous rattlesnakes. But as I promised in the last chapter, that's not going to happen. So relax. Nothing to worry about.

🦌

"Hey, guess what!" Mrs. McDonald said. "The National Museum of Nuclear Science and History is right here in Albuquerque. Ben, we could gather some information for that novel you're planning to write about the Trinity Site."

"Bo-ring!"

Dr. McDonald pulled over to the curb, stopped the car, and turned around to face the twins. They braced for a stern lecture. But their father didn't look angry.

"Look," he said, "you kids are thirteen now. You've

matured a lot on this trip. I can see it. You don't have to be with Mommy and Daddy *all* the time. Your mother and I are going to the Nuclear Science and History Museum. You can come with us, or you can go to the Rattlesnake Museum, or do whatever you want. It's up to you. But I don't want to hear any whining in the backseat."

Coke and Pep looked at each other, communicating silently, as only twins can.

"We'll go to the Rattlesnake Museum," Pep said.

Their parents gave them some money and dropped them off on San Felipe Street, right near the main square in the Old Town section of Albuquerque.

The sign on the little adobe building read RATTLE-SNAKE MUSEUM AND GIFT SHOP. It's a tiny, three-room, mom-and-pop sort of place, but it's packed floor-to-ceiling with the largest collection of live rattlesnakes in the world. Western diamondbacks, black-tails, Mexican lance-headed rattlesnakes, you name it. There are also glass cases filled with tarantulas, scorpions, turtles, and Gila monsters.

Coke took a step back after walking in the door.

"This place is not for herpetophobes," he said. Pep refused to give her brother the satisfaction of explaining what a herpetophobe was.

"Okay, I get it," she said. "You don't like snakes."

In addition to the live specimens, the Rattlesnake Museum also has snake-related artwork, toys, games, jewelry, clothing, sculptures, videos, license plates, and posters for movies like *Cobra Woman*.

"Let's check out the gift shop," Coke said after a few minutes of watching the creepy live snakes.

He opened a door with a GIFT SHOP sign over it and held it for Pep to walk through first. It was a dark, empty room, about the size of a small bedroom.

"This can't be right," Pep said.

When the twins turned around to go back inside the museum, the door closed with a loud *click*.

"Hey, this doesn't look like a . . ."

The door was locked. There was no way out.

At that moment, an engine started up and the

"room" they had walked into began to move.

"What's happening?" Pep shouted, almost falling over.

"It's a trap!" Coke yelled as he struggled to make his way to the wall. "We walked right into it!"

It didn't take long to figure out they were in the back of a truck. Somebody was driving them somewhere. But they didn't know who, and they didn't know where.

"Let us *out!*" Pep screamed, banging on the walls with her fists.

The truck drove a mile or so, and then pulled off to the side of a gravel road. It backed up a few feet and stopped, and then the twins felt the floor under them was starting to tilt. One side was rising up.

"It's some kind of a dump truck!" Pep shouted. "They're dumping us!"

Coke tried to brace himself along the wall to avoid sliding down to the bottom. Pep did the same.

"Hold on!" Coke shouted.

The floor reached a forty-five-degree angle and stopped. Then there was a loud *clunk* and the end of the truck—the lower side—fell away. The twins looked down. All they could see was dirt.

"I can't hold on any longer!" Pep shouted.

A few seconds later she let go, sliding across the

floor, out of the opening, and into a pit. It was a little larger than a grave. Coke followed, nearly landing on top of his sister. Neither of them was hurt,  but that was a small consolation. They were trapped. The walls of the pit were almost five feet high. There was no way to climb out.

"Well, howdy, partners."

Coke and Pep looked up to see a man standing at the edge of the pit. He must have been driving the truck. The man was dressed like a cowboy, with the hat, boots, jeans—the works. In one hand he held a canvas sack.

"Who are *you*?" Pep asked breathlessly.

"Jonathan Pain's the name. You can call me John."

"John Wayne?" Pep asked. "Like that old movie star?"

"Not Wayne. *Pain*," sneered John Pain. "Because that's what I inflict on people. No need to remember my name. You can just call me your worst nightmare."

Coke looked around frantically for a way out of the pit.

"Oh, don't bother trying to leave just yet, young feller," said John Pain. "You ain't goin' nowhere till I'm good and ready to let you go."

"Why are you doing this?" Pep asked. "We never did anything to you."

"Never said you did," John Pain drawled. "But I got two jobs to do this week. The first one is to get some uranium for my employer. I think you may know him. Dr. Herman Warsaw?"

"So he *is* working on a bomb!" Coke said.

It wasn't just some rumor. It was for real.

"What's your other job?" asked Pep.

"Oh. To kill you."

The twins gulped.

"And how are you going to do that?" Coke asked defiantly.

"Oh, you'll find out. When I'm good and ready," said John Pain. "I'm in no rush. It could be five minutes from now, or it could be tomorrow. Or it could be the next day. But you can bet that I'm going to kill you. And it's gonna to be an awful, painful death."

"I thought cowboys were supposed to be *nice*," Pep said.

"You shouldn't stereotype people, little lady," John Pain said. "Some cowboys *are* nice. Others ain't so nice. I would belong in the ain't-so-nice category."

"If Dr. Warsaw hates us so much, why doesn't he kill us himself?" asked Coke. "Why is he always sending people like you to do the dirty work for him?"

"The good doctor is, shall we say, incapacitated," John Pain told them. "He's in no condition to harm anybody. But I am."

The cowboy took a cigarette from his shirt pocket and skillfully lit it by flicking a match with one hand against the bottom of his boot.

"Cigarettes can kill you," Pep pointed out.

"It's true, little lady," said John Pain. "You know what else can kill you?"

He took the canvas sack he'd been carrying and tossed it into the pit.

"Snakes."

Chapter 13

CRUELTY TO ANIMALS

Well, that just goes to show that you can't believe everything you read in a book. Especially *this* book.

You are *so* gullible!

It's time you learned that people who write fiction are a bunch of liars. In fact, lying is their *job*. If one of them tells you there isn't going to be a snake attack in a story, you can pretty much bet there's going to be a snake attack in that story.

Of *course* there was going to be a snake attack! How could there *not* be a snake attack? Didn't they teach you about foreshadowing in school? There was no reason to have Coke and Pep see a sign warning them about snakes if there wasn't going to be a snake attack later on.

🦌

The canvas sack that John Pain tossed into the pit began to slither toward the twins.

"Snakes!" Coke yelled, backing against the dirt wall. "Why did it have to be snakes?"

After wriggling around for a few seconds, a brownish head popped out of the sack's opening. The snake seemed to have enlarged scales at the top of its head and a light stripe behind the corner of its mouth. It opened that mouth ridiculously wide and flicked a forked tongue out. Two sharp fangs were visible. Pep gasped.

"I'd like you to meet Herman," said John Pain. "He's a Mojave rattlesnake. I named him after my good friend Dr. Herman Warsaw."

Herman slithered all the way out of the canvas sack and began to explore the pit. He was about three feet long, with a greenish-brown diamond pattern along his back. Coke and Pep jumped to get out of his way.

"Did you know that seven thousand people are

bitten by venomous snakes in the United States each year?" asked John Pain.

"Venomous?" asked Coke. He was sweating profusely.

"Oh yeah," said John Pain. "The Mojave rattlesnake is the most potently venomous snake in the United States."

"Great."

Herman slithered to the other end of the pit. The twins jumped over him to get as far away as possible.

"Help!" Pep screamed uselessly. "Somebody help!"

"Herman's lookin' for food, I reckon," John Payne said, ignoring her. "You might wanna keep still. His vision ain't so hot, but he's really good at perceivin' movement."

"You're crazy!" Coke yelled.

"Herman also has a keen sense of smell, and a set of heat-sensin' pits in his face that help 'im locate prey," John Pain said casually. "He's got such a big appetite, he only eats once every two weeks."

"When did he eat last?" Pep asked.

"'Bout two weeks ago, I reckon."

"Help!" Pep screamed again. "Somebody help!"

The twins cowered in the corner while Herman explored the other end of the pit.

"He's lyin' in wait, y'see," said John Pain. "When he finds somethin' that looks tasty, like *you*, he'll shake his rattle as a warning, and then pounce. Grab you with them fangs of his. That's how he injects his hemo-toxic venom. It'll travel through your bloodstream—"

"Shut up!" Coke hollered. "Why do you lunatics always have to explain how you're going to kill people?"

"'Cause that's half the fun, son," John Pain said. "After Herman bites ya, you'll feel a tinglin' sensation at first, and you'll start in sweatin'. As the venom destroys yer body tissue, you'll feel weakness and nausea. You may throw up. There'll be swellin', internal bleedin', and intense pain. I love pain. You know what they say—no pain, no gain."

"We gotta get out of here," Coke muttered.

"A few minutes after he bites you, you'll have paralysis and heart failure," John Pain said. "By then, of course, you're a goner."

Herman turned around. It looked like he was eyeing the twins.

"Coke, *do* something!" Pep yelled.

"What do you want *me* to do?"

"I don't know!" Pep shouted. "Didn't you take karate for five years?"

"Are you crazy? Karate moves on a *snake*?"

Herman was on the move again, slithering back and forth.

"After its prey is dead," John Pain continued, "the Mojave rattlesnake eats the head first. It'll even digest the bones. Amazin' creature, when you think about it."

Herman hissed and made a rattle sound with his tail.

"He's about to strike!" Pep screamed.

"Tell you what," John Pain said. "If you two can figure a way outta this mess, I'll let you go. How's that for fair?"

"Quick!" Pep yelled to her brother. "Do you have anything in your pockets? Maybe we can stab him with something."

Coke searched his pockets. The only thing he came up with was the package of freeze-dried ice cream from the Very Large Array Visitor Center. Frantically, he ripped the package open and sprinkled the contents on the ground around Herman.

Herman didn't seem interested.

"Snakes like to eat *livin'* things, pardner," John Pain said, amused. "Like birds and mice and lizards. They don't eat freeze-dried ice cream."

Herman made the rattling sound again.

"I'm going to have to kill it with my bare hands!" Coke said.

"That's a knee-slapper!" John Pain said, doubled over laughing.

"Kill it?" said Pep. "I'm against cruelty to animals. I did a report in school—"

"It's him or us!" Coke shouted. "Somebody's gonna die here!"

Herman moved toward the twins.

"I think he likes you," John Pain said.

"Take your shirt off!" Pep yelled at her brother.

"What? And do *what* with it?"

"I have an idea," Pep said, grabbing the canvas sack from the ground behind Herman. Just give me your shirt!"

Coke pulled his shirt over his head and handed it to his sister. She put it around her neck. Then she held up the canvas bag, with the opening facing Herman.

"What are you *doing*?" Coke asked. "Are you out of your mind?"

"Maybe," Pep said softly.

She was moving the sack back and forth slowly, like a bullfighter taunting a bull. Herman raised his head slightly, moving it left to right as if it was trying to get a better view. Pep's fingertips were trembling.

"Careful," Coke said.

And then, in a flash, Herman rattled his tail and jabbed his head forward to strike at Pep. He hit the center of the sack with his face and Pep quickly closed it around his head. Then she took Coke's T-shirt and wrapped it around the end of the sack, tying a tight knot. Herman's head was trapped inside while the rest of his body was sticking out of the sack.

"Nice!" Coke shouted. "Did you learn that in Girl Scouts?"

Pep grabbed Herman at his middle. Then she swung him like a baseball bat against the side of the pit.

Coke's eyes bugged out. He had never seen his sister do *anything* as aggressive as that. Up until this moment, *he* was usually the one who got them out of these situations. *He* was the one who forced them to jump off the cliff back in California. *He* was the one who gave the boot to Dr. Warsaw back in Wisconsin.

After she smashed Herman's head into the rocks, Pep turned around and swung him against the *other* side of the pit.

Her eyes were on fire now. She was in a frenzy, slamming the rattler from one side of the pit to the other. Poor Herman didn't have a chance. But Pep just kept going, grunting with each swing.

"Stop! Pep!" Coke finally shouted at her. "Stop! He's dead!"

Pep whacked Herman a few more times for good measure. Then, panting, she let go of the sack and fell against the ground. There were tears in her eyes.

"Wow!" her brother exclaimed. "I thought you said

you were against cruelty to animals."

"I don't know what came over me," Pep said, still gasping and sobbing. "I killed a living thing! It wasn't some bad guy. It wasn't a robot. It was alive, and now it's dead because of what I did. It was an instinct, or adrenaline, or something."

"It was *awesome*," Coke said, putting his arm around his sister.

Up above, at the edge of the pit, John Pain clapped his hands in appreciation.

"Impressive!" he said, reaching down to help the twins climb out of the pit. "You're almost as sadistic as I am, young lady."

"So you'll let us go?" Pep asked.

"I'm a man of my word," John Pain said. "I said if you got outta this mess, you'd be free to go. So ske-daddle! But needless to say, if your parents find out about this, I'll kill them."

"Don't worry," Pep told him. "Our parents don't believe anything we tell them anyway."

"Let's blow this pop stand!" Coke said.

The twins took off before John Pain had the chance to change his mind. As they were running away, he shouted to them, "But you two ain't seen the last of me, I promise you that."

Chapter 14

THE OLD HOPI

Coke and Pep ran. They just *ran*. They didn't know where. It didn't matter. Anywhere. Away from that lunatic, John Pain.

"That guy was nuts!" Pep said after a couple of blocks. She stopped to catch her breath.

"I can't believe you killed the snake!" Coke said.

"I can't believe *you* tried to feed it freeze-dried ice cream!"

Across the street, a lady was pushing a stroller. Coke jogged over to ask her how to get back to Albuquerque's Old Town section. She pointed out the direction, and from there it wasn't hard for the twins to find the Rattlesnake Museum. Their parents were standing out front, looking worried.

"Where's your shirt?" asked an exasperated Mrs. McDonald as soon as she saw her son.

Not *Where have you been?* or *Are you okay?* His mother's overriding concern was with what happened to Coke's shirt.

"Funny you should ask, Mom," he replied. "Pep wrapped it around a rattlesnake's head so she could beat it to death."

"Very funny," said Dr. McDonald.

"It's true," Pep insisted. "You don't have to believe him if you don't want to."

Mrs. McDonald simply shook her head, counting how many perfectly good T-shirts Coke had ruined on the trip so far. Five? Six? She had finally reached the point where she wasn't going to fight about it anymore. There was no use. The boy was a T-shirt-wrecking machine. She made a mental note to buy him only cheap T-shirts from now on.

Go to Google Maps (http://maps.google.com/).

Click Get Directions.

In the A box, type Albuquerque NM.

In the B box, type Lupton AZ.

Click Get Directions.

The McDonalds had a quick dinner and checked into the Econo Lodge West for the night. It was just a few blocks from Coronado Freeway—also known as I-40—which was the main road heading west out of Albuquerque. In the morning, the family got on the road early. It would be a long day, in more ways than one.

Almost immediately, the highway flattened out. The stores and gas stations became few and far between. Pep worried silently, trying to figure out where Dr. Warsaw might decide to set off his nuclear bomb, and what they could do to stop it. Coke daydreamed, thinking about John Pain and the last thing he'd said to them: "You two ain't seen the last of me, I promise you that."

There wasn't much to look at out the window, except for the occasional billboard, announcing things like INDIAN VILLAGE and MOCCASINS FOR THE ENTIRE FAMILY!

"Ooh, can we go?" Pep asked.

"Those places aren't *real* Indian villages," Mrs. McDonald told them. "It says in the guidebook that they're just tacky souvenir shops."

"Ooh, can we go?" Coke asked.

About an hour from Albuquerque, the speed limit slowed down to 35 miles per hour and a few stores popped up here and there. And then this appeared at the side of the road. . . .

"That's right!" Dr. McDonald said, slapping his forehead. "I forgot all about it. This is the Great Divide!"

Dear reader, if you recall *The Genius Files: Mission Unstoppable*, you know the McDonalds first crossed the Continental Divide heading east through Utah. It's an imaginary boundary line that begins in Alaska and continues all the way down through South America. Now they were crossing it again, heading west.

"Rivers on the west side of this line flow into the Pacific Ocean," Dr. McDonald reminded the others, "and the rivers on the east side of the line flow into the Atlantic Ocean."

"That's cool," Pep said.

"I read somewhere," said her brother, "that when you flush a toilet in the northern hemisphere, the water swirls in the opposite direction than a toilet flushed in the southern hemisphere."

"That's one of those urban legends," his father told him. "It's totally not true."

"It *sounds* like it could be true."

"Trust me, it's not."

"Who *cares* which direction toilet water swirls?" Pep asked. "And what does that have to do with the Continental Divide?"

Nothing, of course. But you know what, reader? Sometimes people talk about nonsense. Especially people who have been cooped up in a car for four weeks.

Clustered on the road around the Continental Divide were several "Indian Villages" selling rubber tomahawks, purses, belts, hats, and "kachina dolls," whatever they were.

"Pull over, Ben!" Mrs. McDonald shouted.

"Why, Bridge?" he replied, hitting the brakes.

"I have to go to the bathroom," said Pep.

"I want to get a snack," said Coke.

"We need to buy some T-shirts for Coke," said Mrs. McDonald.

Reluctantly, Dr. McDonald pulled over.

Indian Market was a pretty standard souvenir shop, stuffed with bins full of cheap trinkets that most people regret buying as soon as they get home. Dr. McDonald refused to have any part of such nonsense, and he said he would wait in the car while the rest of the family wasted their time and money. Pep went inside to use the bathroom. Mrs. McDonald checked out the T-shirts. Coke walked around look-ing at the knickknacks. Several employees eyed him suspiciously, as storekeepers do when teenage boys enter their place of business.

Most of the employees didn't look like Native Americans at all. But one of them did. He was an old man sitting in the corner, carving a piece of wood with a pocket knife. Next to him on a table were some painted wooden dolls, decorated with feathers and outfitted with brightly colored costumes.

"I am Hopi," the man said to Coke. "Every year our spirits—the kachinas—come down to the villages to dance and sing. They bring rain for the harvest and give gifts to the children. We carve these dolls in the likeness of the kachinam. You want to buy one?"

"No, thank you," Coke said politely. "But they are very beautiful."

He started to walk away, but the old man grabbed him by the elbow.

"Wait," he said. "There is something I need to tell you."

Coke rolled his eyes. The last thing in the world that he needed was a kachina doll. But he didn't want to be rude to the old man.

"What?" he asked, pulling his arm away.

"Forty-nine minutes and eight seconds," whispered

the man. "Twenty-eight minutes and forty point five seconds."

"Huh?" Coke replied. "Excuse me?"

"Listen," the man said, looking into Coke's eyes. "This is *very* important. Did you hear me? I said forty-nine minutes and eight seconds. Twenty-eight minutes and forty point five seconds."

"So what?" Coke asked. "What's that supposed to mean?"

"Write it down," said the man.

"I don't *need* to write it down," Coke said. "Leave me alone."

"Here, I'll write it down for you."

Coke hurried away from the Hopi man and walked out the front door. Pep was waiting for him there.

"Who was that guy you were talking to?" she asked.

"Some old dude who lost his marbles," Coke told her. "He kept saying the same thing over and over again. 'Forty-nine minutes and eight seconds. Twenty-eight minutes and forty point five seconds.' The guy is probably senile or something."

"He's not senile!" Pep said. "Can't you see? It's another cipher!"

"You gotta be kidding me," said Coke. "Forty-nine minutes and eight seconds. Twenty-eight minutes and forty point five seconds. What could that possibly mean?"

"It has something to do with time, obviously," Pep said.

"Sure, but what?"

"Mom, can we borrow your laptop?" Pep asked once they were in the car and back on I-40 West.

She clicked on Google and had her brother type in "49 minutes and 8 seconds. 28 minutes and 40.5 seconds."

The first thing that came up was a list of high scores for the computer game Halo. The next few hits were about the TV show *Glee*.

"Try forty-nine point zero eight," Pep suggested.

Coke tried it. "49.08" turned out to be part of the Texas penal code. Apparently, there are severe penalties if you kill somebody while driving drunk in Texas.

"It doesn't mean *anything*," Coke muttered. "That old guy was just senile, like I said."

"It means *something*," Pep insisted. "The ciphers always tie together somehow. We just have to figure out how."

She added the new entry into her notepad . . .

CIPHER #1: MAY 28, 1937, VOLKSWAGEN
IS FOUNDED
CIPHER #2: 49:08. 28:40.5

Mrs. McDonald showed Coke some new T-shirts she had bought for him, and they had a brief argument over whether or not they were cool enough to wear in public. Soon they were driving through the town of Gallup, New Mexico, which is nicknamed "Indian Capital of the World" because three tribes call the surrounding area their home.

"Hey, it says here that a movie was filmed in Gallup," said Mrs. McDonald. "Maybe we should stop and look around."

"What movie?" asked Dr. McDonald.

"*Natural Born Killers.*"

"Keep driving!" the twins shouted.

The family rode in silence for the next twenty miles until they came to this. . . .

Go to Google Maps (http://maps.google.com).

Click Get Directions.

In the A box, type Lupton AZ.

In the B box, type Sedona AZ.

Click Get Directions.

Chapter 15
YOUR FUTURE WILL COME

"Woo hoo!" Coke hooted as the Ferrari crossed the border. "The Grand Canyon State, baby!"

Outside, Arizona didn't look all that different from New Mexico. Mesas—or were they plateaus?—lined both sides of the road. A truck stop called Speedy's was quickly followed by the Tee Pee Trading Post and a line of other souvenir shops hawking cheap jewelry and moccasins. But even so, just crossing another state line made everyone feel like they were just a little bit closer to home.

"How much farther do we have to go, Mom?" Pep

called from the backseat.

Mrs. McDonald looked it up on her laptop.

"Nine hundred and fifty-eight miles," she reported.

"A hop, skip, and a jump," said Dr. McDonald as he continued on I-40 West.

Mrs. McDonald dropped her New Mexico guidebook in the trash and opened a new one—*Arizona Arisin'*. She flipped through the introduction. . . .

"Let's see . . . soaring mountains . . . red-walled canyons . . . vast deserts . . . ," she mumbled. "Hey, did you guys know that Arizona has more mountains than Switzerland and more golf courses than Scotland?"

"I suppose you're going to tell us about all the oddball museums and weird stuff there is to see here, huh, Mom?" asked Coke.

"Well, the official state neckwear is the bolo tie," Mrs. McDonald said. "In fact, there's a bolo tie museum close to Phoenix."

"Please say we don't have to go there," Pep begged from the backseat. *"Please?"*

"You guys are no fun," said Mrs. McDonald. "Hey, you want to go to London Bridge?"

"Isn't London Bridge in *London*?" asked Coke.

Actually, it is and it isn't. There are several London Bridges. But one of them was sinking into the Thames

River so England put it up for sale in 1967. An American bought it, and he had all 10,246 bricks shipped to Lake Havasu, Arizona, to be reassembled there.

"London Bridge is on the other side of the state, five hours from here," said Mrs. McDonald.

"I'm not driving five hours to see a *bridge*," said Dr. McDonald. "I want to see *natural* beauty. I want to see the Grand Canyon, the red sandstone at Sedona, Monument Valley . . ."

Forty minutes after crossing the state line, they were still arguing about what to see in Arizona. That's when they came to this sign. . . .

Dr. McDonald pulled into the parking lot at the visitors' center. It was at least a hundred degrees outside, and Mrs. McDonald made sure everyone had a bottle of water and was covered by sunglasses, hats, and sunscreen. A park ranger was just starting a short walking tour, so the McDonalds rushed to catch up.

The Petrified Forest isn't a "forest" in the common use of the word. It's more of a rock garden, with spectacular colors. That's why part of the Petrified Forest is called the Painted Desert.

"I don't get it," Pep said to the ranger. "If this is a forest, where are the trees?"

"We get that question all the time," said the ranger, a tall man with blond hair. "Usually when a tree falls, it decays over time. But these trees fell into rivers and were buried in water, minerals, and volcanic ash. So they remained intact and became fossilized. That is, they turned to stone. Some of them are two hundred and twenty-five million years old."

Mrs. McDonald took some notes for *Amazing but True.* After a short walk, the ranger stopped and knelt down to point out a flat rock that had a picture of an eye carved into it.

"Graffiti?" somebody asked.

"You might say that," said the ranger. "These pictures are called petroglyphs. Prehistoric people made them over eight thousand years ago."

Everyone got down on their hands and knees to

examine the petroglyph. There were others depicting a squatting man, a caterpillar, a ladder, and a spoked wheel.

"What do they mean?" Pep asked.

"There are lots of theories," the ranger told her. "They might have been primitive maps, or astronomical markers. Or maybe they were religious symbols, or boundaries between different tribes. We really don't know for sure."

Pep, always interested in codes and secret messages, was fascinated by the petroglyphs. Her brother—he of the short attention span—had wandered a short distance away from the group. He happened to look down to see a large gray rock with these letters written on it. . . .

EDIWEFER

Coke called his sister over.

"Look at this," he said. "The ancient people couldn't have known English, could they?"

"Of course not."

Pep knelt down and touched one of the letters with one finger. It rubbed off. The message appeared to be written in chalk. Clearly, it was recent. A good rain would have washed those letters away.

"What do you think?" Coke asked.

"I think it's another cipher," Pep replied.

So now there were three . . .

CIPHER #1: MAY 28, 1937, VOLKSWAGEN IS FOUNDED
CIPHER #2: 49:08. 28:40.5
CIPHER #3: EDIWEFER

Or whatever *that* meant. Pep couldn't see the solution right away, and the heat was making it hard to concentrate on the cipher. The twins rejoined the group, which was heading back to the visitors' center.

Someone was trying to tell them something, that was for sure. Probably Dr. Warsaw. When they got back in the car, Pep turned to a clean page in her notepad and wrote it down. . . .

EDIWEFER

Why did Dr. Warsaw have to use codes and ciphers all the time? Pep wondered. *If he has a message to get across, why doesn't he just say it?*

An hour later, Pep was still trying to decipher EDI-WEFER when her father pulled off I-40 in Winslow, Arizona, so he could stand on a corner there and sing the old Eagles song "Take It Easy." They had lunch at a little sandwich shop there, and then drove another half hour west until they reached someplace called Meteor Crater. Coke assumed it was a phony tourist trap, but in fact it's an actual crater in the middle of the desert that's nearly a mile across, 2.4 miles around, and 500 feet deep.

Fifty thousand years ago, an asteroid slammed into the earth at this spot to create a gigantic hole in the ground. Mrs. McDonald dutifully took notes for *Amazing but True*. Pep celebrated the event by purchasing a Meteor Crater Frisbee in the gift shop.

After that, it was just forty-five minutes west to Flagstaff, Arizona, and another forty-five minutes south on Route 89A to Sedona. The plan was to spend the rest of the day and the night there. Mrs. McDonald had booked a room at the Days Inn.

Sedona is one of the prettiest towns in the West, mainly because of the red sandstone formations that seem to glow at night when the sun goes down. The locals have given them intriguing names, like Cathedral Rock and the Devil's Kitchen.

But Mrs. McDonald didn't want to come to Sedona for the natural beauty. She wanted to see and experience the Sedona energy vortexes.

The *what*?

A "vortex" is a funnel shape created by a whirling fluid or the motion of spiraling energy. There are four of these swirling centers of energy coming from the surface of the earth in and around Sedona. They're sort of spiritual power centers. Energy saturates the area, and strengthens the inner being of each person who is at a vortex point.

Or so some people believe, anyway.

"That's a lot of bull, Mom," said Coke.

"You kids don't have to come to the vortex," Mrs. McDonald told him. "Your father and I can go on our own."

So they did. Their parents drove off to groove on the vibes at Bell Rock Vortex while the twins hung around the hotel room watching *SpongeBob* reruns.

An hour later, Coke was getting antsy and suggested taking a walk. Having seen every *SpongeBob* episode at least ten times, Pep agreed.

As the twins left the hotel and walked down the main drag, they looked at the storefront windows—Crystal Magic, Sedona School of Massage, Mystical Bazaar, Peace Place, Anti-Aging Life Extension, Center for the New Age Metaphysical Superstore . . .

"Gee, this is sort of a hippie town," Pep noted.

A few blocks down, they stopped in front of a little house with a sign out front that said PSYCHIC COUNSELOR & HEALER. At the bottom of the sign were the words SEE YOUR FUTURE . . . TODAY.

Pep pushed her face against the window so she could peek inside. There was a woman sitting on a couch with her eyes closed, as if she was meditating. She had long black hair and flowing robes.

"Hey, let's go in here," Pep said.

"Are you crazy?" Coke replied. "These people just take your money."

"Come on, it'll be fun," Pep said. "Maybe she really *can* see our future. And tell us what's going to happen to us."

"I can't believe people buy into that stuff," said Coke.

"Hey, neither of us believed in aliens until a couple of days ago," his sister pointed out.

"I have a bad feeling about this," Coke said as his sister pulled open the door. "Hold on to your wallet."

"You and your feelings!"

The bell on the door jingled softly, and the psychic healer lady opened her eyes and smiled. There were colorful tapestries and peace signs covering the walls. The smell of burning incense filled the small room.

"Come. Sit," the woman said, patting the couch next to her. "Heal your hearts. Allow me to help you find your spiritual direction, fulfill your greatest potential, and create a more successful life path."

Coke rolled his eyes. This lady *had* to be kidding.

"We want to know our future," Pep said as she sat on the couch. "It's very important."

"You have come to the right place," the lady told her. "Your spirit guides will give you insight and direction or clarify your path and manifest your dreams."

"How much is this gonna cost?" Coke griped.

"There will be no charge. Sit down, please."

Coke sat on the couch.

"Do you need to hold our hands or anything?" Pep asked.

"That won't be necessary," the woman said. "Just focus on the eternal. Your future will come."

She closed her eyes.

"Together we must release your emotional blocks caused by shame, guilt, and fear," she said softly. "It is the only way to provide guidance for a brighter tomorrow. I am letting the energy flow into you and through you, so that I might understand your true path."

"Oh, geez," Coke said. "What a load of—"

"Can you tell us anything *specific*?" Pep asked.

"Yes," the woman said. "I see a troubled man in your life."

Pep's eyes opened wide. She looked at her brother.

"That's a lucky guess," Coke said. "Anybody could have come up with that."

"The troubled man has been pursuing you," the woman said.

"That's true!" Pep exclaimed.

"Oh yeah?" Coke said. "If you know so much, what's this troubled man's name?"

"He is a sick, sick man," said the woman. "Sick in the head, not in the body."

"Ha!" Coke said. "That proves it. You don't know his name. You're a fraud."

"I see a city in Poland," said the woman. "The capital."

"Warsaw!" Pep shouted. "Warsaw is the capital of

Poland! Dr. Warsaw is the man who's chasing us!"

Even Coke was impressed by *that*. Maybe the woman *was* psychic.

"Dr. Warsaw has been chasing you for a long time . . . all the way across the country," the woman said. "You are almost home now, yes? You are heading west. To California. I see another man. Pain."

"That's John Pain!" Coke said excitedly. "He tried to kill us with a rattlesnake!"

"Where is Dr. Warsaw going to set off his nuclear bomb?" Pep begged. "We have to know. Tell us what else you see! Is he going to kill us? Please!"

The woman closed her eyes again. Both twins looked at her imploringly for answers. Even if they were going to die at the hands of Dr. Warsaw, there might be some comfort in knowing how much time they had left.

There was something vaguely familiar about the psychic woman's face. Tufts of short brown hair peeked out between strands of her long black hair. Coke glanced down and noticed a chocolate bar and a bottle of hand sanitizer on the table next to her. He looked at her face again, more carefully. That's when he knew. He leaned over and yanked the wig off her head.

"Mrs. Higgins!" both twins yelled.

Yes, it was Audrey Higgins, their germaphobic, chocoholic health teacher, and Dr. Warsaw's hench-man and ex-fiancée!

"I no longer go by that name," said Mrs. Higgins calmly. "Now I am Aurora Moonbeam."

"You're an assassin!" Coke shouted, pointing his finger at her face. "I don't care *what* you call yourself."

"Please," Mrs. Higgins said. "Those days are behind me. I've changed. I am a peaceful, loving person now. You've got to believe me."

"Believe you?" Pep yelled. "You locked us in the detention room and then set our school on fire! You tried to kill us at The House on the Rock. You tried to blow our ears out at the Rock and Roll Hall of Fame. You poisoned our bowling shoes in Texas!"

"And don't forget about Wrigley Field!" Coke added.

"Each time we trusted you, and each time you tried to kill us again," Pep yelled. "I will *never* believe you! I will *never* trust you!"

Both twins were on their feet now, shouting at Mrs. Higgins. She looked small and helpless sitting on the couch. Her eyes were watery.

"I was in love with Herman Warsaw," she whim-pered. "That's why I did all those horrible things to you. It was for love. We were going to be married. I know everything I did was wrong now. I know I deceived you. I'm wracked with guilt. What can I do to make it up to you? I'll do *anything*."

"It's all an act, Pep," Coke said. "She's doing it again. Don't fall for it."

Pep *wasn't* falling for it. Not this time. Pep was furious. Her eyes were on fire.

"You still love him!" she said to Mrs. Higgins. "You'll *always* love him!"

"I will," she admitted. "But he's insane now. He's too far gone. Herman is incapable of loving another person. So I'm finished with him. Why won't you believe me?"

At that point, she broke down sobbing. It was hard to watch. And quite convincing. Coke was starting to waver. Maybe Mrs. Higgins *had* changed.

But Pep wasn't buying it.

"Save the tears, you phony!" she shouted. "I'm not falling for them. Not *this* time."

With that, Pep leaped on the couch and attacked Mrs. Higgins, punching her and kicking her. Coke was so shocked that all he could do was stand back and watch as his sister pummeled the helpless woman. Mrs. Higgins wasn't even fighting back. All she could do was put her hands in front of her face to try to ward off the blows. Tears rolled down her cheeks as she sobbed pathetically.

"Pep! Stop it!" Coke finally shouted as he pulled his sister away. "Get off her! Are you out of your mind?"

Chapter 16

CHOICE POINT

Something had come over Pep McDonald. Four weeks earlier, she had been a pretty normal California girl, concerned with her homework, babysitting, and soccer. But in the last two days alone, she had beaten up a defenseless woman and killed a snake with her bare hands. She had gained a tremendous amount of confidence, and ruthlessness. It was like she was a different person.

Her brother, on the other hand, seemed to have lost some of the swagger he'd displayed at the start of the trip. Coke was no longer calling himself "Ace Fist" and bragging about his karate skills. He had become hesitant, tentative, sometimes hanging back and letting his sister take charge of the situation.

The pressure of being chased and hunted down like animals over thousands of miles was starting to wear on both of the twins. Knowing that Dr. Warsaw was building an atomic weapon and might set it off at any time had frayed their nerves. They were less than 800 miles from San Francisco now. Questions were running through the backs of their minds. *Will we get home alive? What's going to happen if we do? Will we be able to live a normal life? Will we be hunted—and haunted—by Dr. Warsaw forever?*

The uncertainty was eating at them.

"I don't know what happened," Pep said on the way back to the hotel. "I think I just snapped."

Coke flipped on the TV to help them both calm down. *SpongeBob* was on again. A few minutes later, there was a knock on the door. Their parents were back.

"Oh, I wish you kids had come to the vortex with us!" gushed Mrs. McDonald. "I felt the energy. The hair on my arms was standing on end!"

"Personally, I didn't feel a thing," said Dr. McDonald. "I say it's all a hoax."

"You're still sitting here watching TV?" asked Mrs.

McDonald. "You kids haven't moved an inch since we left."

"Actually, we went out for a walk," Coke said. "We consulted with a psychic healer, and then Pep beat her up."

"Ha! You kids are a riot," said his father. "I guess that healer wasn't really psychic, because if she was, she would have known that Pep was going to beat her up, right?"

They went to eat at a little Italian restaurant down the street. After dinner, Dr. McDonald called a family meeting. He had read an article in a magazine that said children enjoy and appreciate family vacations better when they're involved in the decision-making process. Up until this point, the parents had pretty much decided where they were going, and the kids had had no say in the matter.

"We are *here*," Dr. McDonald said, after spreading his road map across the table and pointing to Sedona, Arizona. "We have two choices tomorrow. We can drive south down to Phoenix or north up to the Grand Canyon."

"What's in Phoenix?" Pep asked.

"Oh, there's lots of cool stuff," Mrs. McDonald said as she pulled out her Arizona guidebook. "Let me see. There's the Musical Instrument Museum, and the Hall of Flame Museum of Firefighting. Oh, and there's also the Phoenix Police Museum. They have a room honoring police dogs that have died in the line of duty. And you get to sit inside a real police car."

"That sounds pretty cool," Coke said.

"Wait, listen to *this*!" said Mrs. McDonald after flipping the page. "There's a Cockroach Hall of Fame!"

"You gotta be kidding me," Coke said.

"It's true," his mother continued. "An exterminator has a place called the Pest Shop. In the back, he made a museum with dead cockroaches dressed as celebrities!"

"That's ridiculous, Bridge," said Dr. McDonald.

"Oh, come on!" Mrs. McDonald told him. "It will be fun! It says they have David Letteroach, Marilyn Monroach, Liberoachi, and roach versions of Elvis, Britney Spears, and lots of other famous people. Oh, we *must* go!"

Dr. McDonald closed his eyes and rubbed his forehead silently. He had already endured museums devoted to yo-yos, hot dog buns, mustard, bowling, washing machines, and Spam on this trip. He tried to think of a diplomatic way to get out of driving 117 miles to see costumed cockroaches.

"I think the children would get more out of a trip to the Grand Canyon," he said gently.

"The Grand Canyon is just a big hole in the ground," Mrs. McDonald replied. "What's the big deal about *that*?"

"It's one of the seven natural wonders of the world!" her husband said, raising his voice somewhat.

"I'm just kidding, Ben," Mrs. McDonald said. "The Grand Canyon and Phoenix are both about two hours from here. How about we let the kids decide which direction we go?"

"Fair enough."

While their parents went to pay the check for dinner, Coke and Pep stayed at the table and talked things over.

"Do you care where we go?" Pep asked.

"No."

"Me neither," Pep said. "The important thing is, where are Dr. Warsaw and his pals likely to go? If we go to Phoenix and they go to the Grand Canyon, we avoid them, at least for a while. If we go to Phoenix and *they* go to Phoenix, we're in trouble. We've got to outguess them."

"Of course, they could track us and follow us *anywhere*," Coke pointed out. "Dr. Warsaw could be watching us right *now*."

The twins debated the issue a little while longer, and then joined their parents at the cash register.

"We vote for the Grand Canyon," Pep said.

"Yes!" shouted Dr. McDonald with a fist pump.

🦌

Go to Google Maps (http://maps.google.com/).

Click Get Directions.

In the A box, type Sedona AZ.

In the B box, type Grand Canyon National Park AZ.

Click Get Directions.

In the morning, the McDonalds set out on Route 89A heading north for 24 miles until it merged into I-17, which intersected with I-40 West. Just before the town of Williams, Dr. McDonald took exit 165 for Route 64, which goes directly north for 50 miles to Grand Canyon National Park. You can follow it on the map.

In the front seat, Dr. McDonald had found a classic rock station on the radio and turned the volume up loud. When Pep tired of looking at the scenery, she absentmindedly pulled out her notepad and realized that she hadn't solved the cipher they received back at the Petrified Forest . . .

EDIWEFER

Pep tried all her usual strategies, but nothing seemed to work. She was frustrated. If she wasn't so stressed out, she figured, she would have cracked the code by now. Maybe EDIWEFER wasn't a cipher at all. Maybe it was just somebody's name.

While she kept juggling the letters around, Coke borrowed his mother's laptop computer. He went online and searched for an anagram solver—a simple program that can take any group of letters and generate every possible word that can be made from those letters. There were several free anagram solvers online, so Coke picked the one at the top of the list and typed in EDIWEFER. Almost instantly, the computer spit out a list. . . .

if reed we

if deer we

fewer die

die fewer

fried ewe

free wide

deer wife

I were fed

I wed reef

ever I fed

I we freed

I reed few

fireweed

"I got it!" Coke said, poking his sister.

"Got what?"

"The answer!" Coke said. "I think EDIWEFER is 'fireweed'!"

"Fireweed?" Pep asked. "What's that? I never heard of fireweed."

"It's a plant," Coke told her. "A wildflower. It's one of the first plants to appear after a forest fire."

"How can you possibly know that?" Pep asked. "Nobody knows that."

"*Lots* of people know that," her brother told her. "You're just not one of them."

"But what does a plant have to do with anything?" Pep asked. "How does that tie in with the other clues?"

"Hey, all I know is that EDIWEFER is very probably 'fireweed.' I can't tell you what it means. That's *your* department."

Pep sighed and updated her list. . . .

CIPHER #1: MAY 28, 1937, VOLKSWAGEN
IS FOUNDED
CIPHER #2: 49:08. 28:40.5
CIPHER #3: FIREWEED

Chapter 17

THE PERFECT PLACE FOR TROUBLE

Pep had been working so hard on EDIWEFER that she hadn't noticed the road led directly into Grand Canyon National Park. It is, of course, one of the most popular tourist destinations in America.

"Did you know," Coke asked the family, "that if you took four skyscrapers that were a thousand feet high and stacked them on top of one another inside the Grand Canyon, they *still* wouldn't reach the rim?"

"Thank you, Mr. Who Cares," Pep said.

"Don't be mean to your brother," said Dr. McDonald.

I know what you're thinking, reader. You're guessing that a *major* scene in this book is going to take place at the Grand Canyon. It's been a few chapters since anyone tried to kill Coke and Pep, and the Grand Canyon would be the *perfect* location for another attempt on their lives.

It's almost *too* perfect. Despite warning signs all over the place, more than five hundred people have died at the Grand Canyon.

Let me count the ways.

There have been lots of hikers who didn't bring enough water and died from dehydration. People have drowned in the Colorado River at the bottom of the canyon after getting caught in a flash flood. People have been struck by lightning and falling boulders. There have been numerous snakebite victims.

Then, of course, there are all the people who have fallen from a ledge. Surprisingly, a number of tourists have died while *posing for photos*. The photographer told them to take a step back, and, well, you can imagine what happened after that. There have even been reports of men who slipped and fell to their deaths while they were merely trying to pee into the canyon. Look it up if you don't believe me. And I haven't even mentioned all the people who died in airplane crashes and freak accidents.

It's a no-brainer, right? It would be so easy for the twins to become separated from their parents and get lost on a hike in the canyon. And then Dr. Warsaw, John Pain, the bowler dudes, or some other lunatic could conveniently be right there to give them a gentle shove over the edge.

But of course Coke and Pep would miraculously survive the fall somehow, right? Coke's T-shirt would rip in the process, and the chapter would end with their clueless mother complaining that he doesn't take better care of his clothes.

That chapter would practically write itself!

Well, forget about it. It didn't happen that way. Remember what I said about assuming things?

That's right, *nobody* dies at the Grand Canyon in this book. No bad guys show up with evil intentions and unnecessarily complicated devices. There aren't any preposterous accidents or incidents.

No, starting at Grand Canyon Village on the South Rim, the twins and their parents have a simply *lovely* time hiking and enjoying the spectacular scenery and multiple switchbacks on the Bright Angel Trail. Then they enjoy a sumptuous dinner at the El Tovar Lodge dining room and a leisurely, restful night's sleep.

Sorry to disappoint you.

By the way, isn't there *enough* mayhem in this story already? I mean, really, you should be ashamed of yourself for hoping to read about somebody trying to kill the twins at the Grand Canyon! Is that all you care about it? What does it say that you get so much pleasure out of the misfortunes of others? You're probably the kind of person who goes to NASCAR races just to see the cars crash into each other.

🦌

Even though there was no attempt on the lives of the twins, something significant *did* happen while Coke and Pep were at the Grand Canyon. The next morning, when they got in the car to leave, Pep opened her notepad and found this. . . .

CIPHER #4:
ATLEDOEMORAHPLAAMILMRO
FINUOVARB

And it was written in someone else's handwriting.

"Did you write this?" Pep asked, showing the page to her brother.

"No," Coke replied.

"It's not Mom's or Dad's handwriting."

The twins looked at the page again, and then at each other.

"Somebody was in our car," they both said.

> Go to Google Maps (http://maps.google.com).
>
> Click Get Directions.
>
> In the A box, type Grand Canyon National Park AZ.
>
> In the B box, type Hoover Dam.
>
> Click Get Directions.

Chapter 18

HOOVER DAM

A shiver went down Pep's back. She was angry, frightened, and just a little freaked out that some creep had broken into their car while the family had been hiking in the canyon. Not only that, but he—or she—had been sitting in her seat, writing in her private notepad, and possibly messing around with her other stuff. *What if somebody put a bomb in their car?* She looked through her backpack to make sure that nothing had been disturbed.

"I have a bad feeling about this," Pep told her brother.

But she didn't mention anything to her parents. Dr. McDonald pulled out of the Grand Canyon Village parking lot and got back on the highway.

There aren't a lot of roads leading into or out of Grand Canyon National Park. To continue heading west, you have to drive south on Route 180 for 50 miles, and then get on I-40. For a while, Dr. McDonald veered off onto historic Route 66 for a change of scenery, but then got back on I-40 at the town of Kingman. From there, he took Route 93, which goes out to the tip of Arizona. If you look on the map, he drove in a big U shape.

It was a long drive, more than three hours, and there wasn't a whole lot to look at along the way. Spectacular mountains were in the distance and there was something beautiful about the desert. But everybody was starting to feel like they just wanted to get home.

Dear reader, in the course of this series, I fear that perhaps I haven't conveyed the mind-numbing boredom that goes with sitting in a car for a 3,000-mile trip across the United States and back again. Needless to say, for most travelers, it's not a nonstop thrill ride of visiting goofy tourist traps, solving indecipherable ciphers, and getting attacked by crazed bad guys every few days. A *real* cross-country trip involves a lot of staring out the window for hours and wondering how long it will be until "we're there." I've taken the liberty of leaving out the boring parts to spare you the drudgery of reading a book that would be as dull as an actual cross-country drive. You're welcome!

To pass the time, Pep examined the strange new handwriting in her notepad. She stared at it for a long time, trying to figure out what it could possibly mean . . .

ATLEDOEMORAHPLAAMILAMILMRO
FINUOVARB

None of her usual intricate strategies seemed to work on this one. After an hour or so, Pep found her eyes feeling heavy, and soon she dozed off, her notepad dropping to her feet.

Coke picked it up and looked at the cipher. Just for the heck of it, he wrote it out backward, something his sister usually tried but had neglected to do this time. . . .

**BRAVOUNIFORMLIMALIMA
ALPHAROMEODELTA**

Coke's eye widened. Wait a minute! There were

words in there! He drew slashes in the obvious places. . . .

BRAVO/UNIFORM/LIMA/LIMA/ALPHA/
ROMEO/DELTA

Then he poked his sister awake.

"I *got* it!" he whispered after she opened her eyes. "Look! There are words in there. And Alpha Romeo is a kind of car. Just like Volkswagen."

Pep took the notepad to see what he had written.

"It's not the car, you dope!" she said. "This is the International Radiotelephony Spelling Alphabet."

"The *what*?"

A - ALPHA	B - BRAVO
C - CHARLIE	D - DELTA
E - ECHO	F - FOXTROT
G - GOLF	H - HOTEL
I - INDIA	J - JULIETT
K - KILO	L - LIMA
M - MIKE	N - NOVEMBER
O - OSCAR	P - PAPA
Q - QUEBEC	R - ROMEO
S - SIERRA	T - TANGO
U - UNIFORM	V - VICTOR
W - WHISKEY	X - X-RAY
Y - YANKEE	Z - ZULU

"It's a simple code the military uses so they can relay messages clearly," Pep told him. "You know how in war movies they're always talking into headsets and saying, 'alpha,' 'bravo,' 'charlie,' and stuff like that? They're using words to represent letters to make sure the person at the other end is hearing them right."

"How do you know that?" Coke asked.

"Everybody knows that," Pep replied.

"I didn't know that," Coke said. "So you're saying that BRAVO means B, and UNIFORM means U . . ."

"Right," Pep said. "And LIMA means L. ALPHA means A. ROMEO means R. And DELTA means D. So BRAVO UNIFORM LIMA LIMA ALPHA ROMEO DELTA is . . . B-U-L-L-A-R-D."

"Are you sure that's right?" Coke asked. "BULLARD?"

"That's what it says," his sister replied. "Now all we need to do is find out what BULLARD means."

"Google it," Coke said.

"Mom!"

Mrs. McDonald handed her laptop back to the twins.

"I'm so pleased to see you kids working hard on your summer homework assignments," she said.

Coke and Pep rolled their eyes at each other. Their parents were hopeless.

Coke did a search for BULLARD. It turned up a company that makes protective equipment, such as hardhats for construction workers and helmets for firefighters.

"Where are they located?" Pep asked, looking over his shoulder.

"Kentucky."

"How could that possibly tie in with Volkswagen?" Pep asked.

"Maybe there's a Volkswagen factory in Kentucky, and they have to wear hardhats," Coke replied.

"They have to wear hardhats in *any* factory," his sister said. "And what could that possibly have to do with the fireweed plant?"

Pep sighed, closed her notepad, and stared out the window. The twins were as confused as ever.

You probably are too, reader. But you know one thing for sure. BULLARD is important. If it weren't, there would have been no reason for somebody to break into the car and write it in Pep's notepad.

She added to her list . . .

CIPHER #1: MAY 28, 1937, VOLKSWAGEN
IS FOUNDED
CIPHER #2: 49:08. 28:40.5
CIPHER #3: FIREWEED
CIPHER #4: BULLARD

"We're going to a *dam*?" Pep asked when Dr. McDonald pulled off at the next exit.

"It's not just *any* dam," said her mother. "It's the biggest dam in the world."

"It's dam big," Dr. McDonald said, chuckling at his little joke.

"It's still a dam," Pep said, unimpressed. "Beavers build dams."

Dr. McDonald followed the Hoover Dam signs until he found the parking lot at the visitors' center.

"We want to take the dam tour," he said with a smirk when he got to the ticket window.

The lady behind the glass had heard so many dam jokes, she gave no reaction at all.

"Which dam tour do you want to take?" she asked.

It turns out there are two dam tours. The Powerplant Tour is a half hour and costs fifteen dollars. You take an elevator down into the power plant and see the huge turbines that turn rushing water into electricity. The Hoover Dam Tour is twice as long and allows you to see more of the labyrinth of tunnels that wind their way throughout the dam's mass of concrete. It costs thirty dollars.

"Thirty bucks for each of us?" Coke said to his father. "Sounds kinda high to me, Dad."

"Four tickets to the Powerplant Tour, please," said Dr. McDonald.

As they followed the signs for the start of the tour,

Coke and Pep noticed the security guards and cameras everywhere. Ever since 9/11, national historic sites like Hoover Dam have been on increased alert against terrorist attacks. The beefed-up security makes some people feel nervous, but it made the twins feel safe. Dr. Warsaw and his flunkies wouldn't dare try to hurt them *here*. Coke and Pep could relax and enjoy themselves for a change.

The family was ushered into a room where they watched a short film that explained how Hoover Dam was built and how it changed America. They learned that the dam, which is actually larger than the Great Pyramid of Cheops in Egypt, generates billions of kilowatt hours of electricity and

distributes billions of gallons of water to people and farms all over the west. Without Hoover Dam, life in this part of the country would be impossible.

When the film ended, the tour guide—a short woman—introduced herself and escorted everyone into an elevator, which took them 530 feet down through the rock wall of the canyon.

"More than three million cubic yards of concrete was used to build the dam," the tour guide informed the group. "That's enough concrete to pave a two-lane highway from San Francisco to New York. If the dam was built in one continuous pour, the concrete would take over a century to cool and harden. That's why it was poured in blocks, some as large as fifty feet square and five feet high."

Dr. McDonald was fascinated, as he always was by technology. Mrs. McDonald took notes for *Amazing but True*. The trivia and statistics pretty much washed over Pep, but Coke absorbed it all, whether he wanted to or not.

The McDonalds exited the elevator to walk through a construction tunnel drilled in the 1930s that led to the Powerplant. It was mostly dark in the tunnel, except for a thin row of lights on both sides. It led to a platform, where visitors could see the guts of the dam—seventeen gigantic, two-story-tall turbines that generate electricity.

"In simple terms," the tour guide explained as she walked through the tunnel, "Hoover Dam holds back Lake Mead, and at regular intervals we release some of the water. The water makes the turbines spin, and that generates electric power. Then the water exits and continues on downstream. Follow me to the Penstock viewing platform so we can watch these babies in action."

But the twins, lagging at the back of their group, never made it to the Penstock viewing platform. Because at that moment, they were grabbed from behind by two men who put knives to their throats.

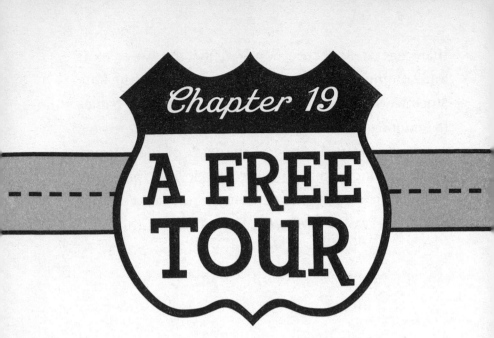

Chapter 19
A FREE TOUR

"**K**eep your mouths shut, or we'll slice your necks
like Wonder Bread."

The whispered voice sounded familiar, but
Coke and Pep weren't about to turn around to find
out who was doing the talking. The twins were pulled
backward through a doorway, and then it slammed
shut. That door led to another tunnel, this one not
open to the public.

Still holding knives to the twins' throats, the two
men dragged Coke and Pep down a long corridor and
through another set of iron doors. It was pitch-dark in

there and perfectly quiet, except the echo of the door slam seemed to go on forever. Pep didn't dare speak. She could hear the sound of her own breathing, and her own heartbeat.

"We got 'em, boss," one of the men grunted.

"Good," said a voice ten feet away. "Now let 'em go. If they try to run, they'll smash their heads into the wall."

"Who *are* you?" Coke demanded after the knife was removed from his neck. "Are you Dr. Warsaw?"

"Nope," the man said simply.

He lit a cigarette with a match, and it illuminated his face just enough to make it partly visible.

"John Pain!" Pep shouted.

"I *told* ya you'd see me again."

Yes, it was John Pain, the long-winded cowboy they had encountered at the Rattlesnake Museum in Albuquerque. He clicked on a flashlight and pointed it at his own face from below. It created an eerie, shadowy image.

"Let us go, Pain!" shouted Pep.

"I *already* let ya go," said John Pain.

"Then let us out of here!" she demanded.

"Oh, I can't do *that*, little lady," Pain said. "I need to finish up the job I started."

"What job was that?" Pep asked.

"Killin' you," John Pain said matter-of-factly. "That was purty clever, the way you took care of that rattlesnake. You really rattled 'im."

The two men who had grabbed Coke and Pep started to giggle like schoolboys.

"Knock it off, you cackling morons!" shouted John Pain, shining his flashlight at them. The two men were dressed like Hoover Dam security guards, except for one thing—they were both wearing bowler-style hats.

"The bowler dudes!" Coke yelled. "Not *again*!"

"At your service!" said the snickering, mustachioed bowler dude. "Long time no see!"

Yes, once again the twins were being hassled by the pair of moronic, sadistic brothers who had already buried them in a sand pit, attacked them with bowling balls, and assisted in several other attempts on their lives over the past five weeks.

"How did you get past security?" Coke asked John Pain.

"We *are* security," he replied.

"Good one, boss," giggled the clean-shaven bowler dude.

"Shut up, you idiot!"

"You want us to kill 'em now?" asked the mustachioed bowler dude.

"That ain't gonna be necessary, boys," Pain drawled.

"Their daddy was too cheap to pay for the full tour, but we're gonna give it to 'em for free. They'll get an exclusive behind-the-scenes look at the insides of the dam."

"We don't want your dam tour!" Pep shouted. "Let us go!"

Both twins thought about making a run for it. But it was so dark in the tunnel, they were sure to injure themselves if they ran into something.

"There are four *trillion* gallons of water in Lake Mead," John Pain informed them. "That's a lot of water pressure."

"We don't care!" Pep barked. "Leave us alone!"

"Oh, you *will* care," Pain said. "'Cause right now we're inside one of the four intake tower pipes of Hoover Dam. It's thirty feet in diameter. At regular intervals, they open a gate and ninety thousand gallons of water comes shootin' through this pipe. That's ninety thousand gallons of water each *second*. It would fill an Olympic-size swimming pool in less than seven seconds."

"Help!" Pep screamed. "Somebody help us!"

"They can't hear you through the concrete," Coke said sadly. There was no fight left in him. He was a beaten man.

"You kids ever been on a waterslide?" asked John

Pain. "This is gonna be a lot like that. Except at the end, you don't land on your fanny in a nice little pool. You land in the spinning turbine of a hydroelectric generator. Ha-ha-ha!"

"Ha-ha, good one, boss," said the clean-shaven bowler dude.

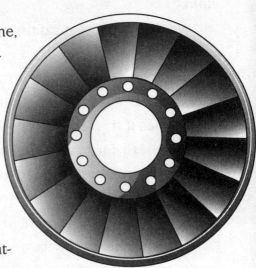

"Quiet!" barked John Pain. "You're ruining my flow."

"Sorry, boss."

"It's an engineering marvel, ain't it?" asked John Pain, pointing the flashlight beam left and right. "The water rushin' through here generates enough 'lectricity to power millions of homes and businesses. And think of it. When your bodies get sliced up by those giant turbine blades, you'll become part of the history. Thanks to you, America will be green. You'll become an alternative source of energy."

The bowler dudes couldn't stop themselves from giggling.

"We're going to die in here!" Pep wailed. "Do something, Coke!"

"What am I supposed to do?" Coke asked.

"Oh, don't feel so bad, little lady," John Pain said. "Lots of folks died right here, buildin' this dam. Ninety-six, to be exact. Legend has it that some of 'em are buried in the concrete and became part of the dam itself. So you'll be in good company."

"You'll never get away with this!" Pep said. She didn't really believe that, but felt the need to say it anyway.

"Lemme tell y'all a little story," Pain said. "The first person to die here was a man named J. G. Tierney, back in 1922. He was a surveyor lookin' for a good spot to build the dam. Poor fella fell into the Colorado River and drowned. And you know who was the *last* man to die here, exactly thirteen years to the day later?"

"Who?" Coke asked.

"His son, Patrick," said John Pain. "He fell from one of the intake towers. True story. Sad story. Makes me kinda tear up, I gotta tell ya."

"You're sick, you know that?" Coke asked. "You need help."

John Pain laughed.

"If anybody needs help, it's y'all," he said as he looked at his watch. "'Cause I reckon that ninety thousand gallons of water is gonna come shootin' down this pipe in . . . about fifty seconds."

"You want me to tie 'em up, boss?" asked one of the bowler dudes.

"Nah, they ain't goin' nowhere," said Pain. "But we really must be taking our leave. Unfortunately, I got me a touch of aquaphobia—fear of water."

The bowler dudes followed John Pain to the door they had used to get inside the giant pipe.

"Wait!" Coke said desperately. "You told us you were going to get uranium for Dr. Warsaw so he could build an atomic bomb. Did you?"

"I most certainly completed that mission," Pain said as he opened the door. "And now I'm gonna complete this one. Ta-ta, y'all. Have a nice life, or what's left of it, anyways."

The door slammed shut. Coke and Pep rushed over and tried to pull it open. No go.

"So Dr. Warsaw *does* have a bomb!" Pep shouted.

"Who cares about that? We're going to *die* in here!" Coke said. "After all we've been through, this is how it ends."

"He was bluffing," Pep assured her brother. "Nothing's gonna happen."

"You're pretty sure of yourself all of a sudden," Coke said. "Ever since you killed that snake."

"Think about it," Pep told him. "How could John

Pain *possibly* know the exact moment when they're going to release the—"

"What's that noise?" Coke shouted.

"What noise?"

"*That* noise!"

Both of them stopped to listen. There was a *whoosh-ing* noise in the distance, echoing off the sides of the pipe. It was getting louder, closer.

"It's the water!" Pep shouted. "It's coming!"

"This is it," Coke said, taking his sister's hand. "This is the end."

"Hang on!" Pep had to shout now to be heard. The pipe was vibrating.

"There's nothing to hang on to!" Coke shouted back.

"We're gonna have to swim!" Pep yelled.

"What, right into the turbine blades?"

They could feel the spray now. The roar of 90,000 gallons of water rushing through the pipe made it impossible to communicate anymore. But Pep tried anyway.

"Hold your breath!" she screamed. "And no matter what happens, I love you!"

There was no point trying to swim. The water swept the two of them up like ping-pong balls and flung them forward. Instinctively, they curled themselves into the fetal position, covering their heads with their hands.

What felt like an eternity took about nine seconds in real time. Coke and Pep rocketed down the pipe on a wave of water, rolling, tumbling, and sliding, upside down and sideways, completely without control.

🦌

Now I know what you're thinking, reader. You're thinking that there's *no way* Coke and Pep could survive the crush of ninety thousand gallons of water and then manage to make it past the blades of a spinning turbine. Surely, they would be drowned, their bones broken, their bodies sliced into tiny pieces. How could they possibly get out of *this* mess?

Well, they did, okay? I can't explain it. I wasn't there. All I can say is that Coke and Pep didn't drown. Their bones weren't broken. Their bodies weren't sliced into tiny pieces. It's preposterous, I know. But hey, that's why you found this book in the fiction section. Miracles happen. Just go with the flow, so to speak.

🦌

Once past the turbine blades, the pipe spit the twins out into the Colorado River downstream from Hoover Dam.

A few seconds later, Pep bobbed to the surface,

choking and gasping for breath. She managed to get her bearings and swim to shore. When she saw her brother nearby, floating face down, she waded back in and grabbed him. Then she pulled him up on a rock and slapped him in the face see if he was conscious.

"Are we dead?" Coke asked, opening his eyes.

"Not yet," Pep told him, panting. "Not yet. Let's blow this pop stand."

Like a couple of drowned rats, the twins struggled to climb up the rocks at the side of the river and back to the visitors' center.

"We've been looking all over for you," Dr. McDonald said when he saw them. "I was about to call the police! You missed most of the tour! What happened?"

"You wouldn't believe us if we told you," Pep said.

"You're soaking wet!" said Mrs. McDonald.

"Hey, at least my shirt isn't ripped," Coke replied.

The twins staggered to the bathroom to change into dry clothes, and soon they were in the Ferrari and on the road again. Dr. McDonald circled back to Route 93 and crossed the Mike O'Callaghan–Pat Tillman Memorial Bridge, which was built in 2010 right next to Hoover Dam. At the end of the bridge, this sign came into view. . . .

Go to Google Maps
(http://maps.google.com).

Click Get Directions.

In the A box, type
Hoover Dam.

In the B box, type
Las Vegas NV.

Click Get Directions.

Chapter 20

VEGAS, BABY!

When she didn't hear any hooting and hollering from the backseat, Mrs. McDonald turned around to look behind her.

"Coke, aren't you going to shout 'Woo-hoo!' and share some Nevada trivia with us?" she asked.

"Woo-hoo," he mumbled, with a total lack of enthusiasm.

"What's the matter, son?" Dr. McDonald asked. "Not feeling well?"

In fact, Coke wasn't feeling well at *all*. Thanks to the incident at Hoover Dam—combined with all the *other* incidents—he was beginning to show classic signs of depression, or maybe learned helplessness. It had finally sunk in with Coke—this is what life was going to be like from now on. Every couple of days, some nutcase would do something horrible to him and his sister.

So far, he and Pep had been lucky. But eventually, one of these attempts on their lives was likely to succeed. It was only a matter of time. They would be dead and Dr. Warsaw would probably kill thousands more with his bomb. That thought would depress anybody.

Besides, there was no reason to hoot and holler about entering Nevada. This was *not* the family's first visit to the state. They'd crossed northern Nevada when they were heading east at the beginning of their trip. Now they were at the southernmost tip of the state on their way back home.

Coke continued to feel glum as the Ferrari headed west on Route 93, also known as The Great Basin Highway. More rocks. More desert. Miles and miles of nothingness. The sun was starting to set, yet the temperature was still close to triple digits.

But then, not more than a half hour after leaving Hoover Dam, signs of civilization started to pop up here and there. At first they were just gas stations and warehouses. But very soon the signs became larger, brighter, and more colorful. The architecture became flashier.

Dr. and Mrs. McDonald knew which city they were approaching, but had decided to surprise the kids. Coke's mood perked up when he spotted this sign. . . .

"Woo-hoo!" he shouted. "Vegas, baby!"

After driving through the desert for almost a week, it was somewhat of a culture shock to see downtown Las Vegas. Everyone was craning their necks as they drove through "the Strip"—four dizzying miles of gigantic hotels, palm trees, flashing lights and signs, wild colors, souvenir shops, magic shows, strange-looking people, and of course, casino after casino.

Most people don't know that the Strip is not *in* the city limits of Las Vegas itself. It's actually in the towns of Winchester and Paradise.

Mrs. McDonald was in paradise herself. She didn't even have to look in her Nevada guidebook to find quirky places to visit in Las Vegas. All she had to do was look out the window. . . .

The Las Vegas Museum of Organized Crime. The Houdini Museum. The Pinball Museum and Hall of Fame. The Elvis-A-Rama Museum. The Neon Museum. There were replicas of the Statue of Liberty and the Eiffel Tower. A dancing waters fountain show outside the Bellagio Hotel. The largest gold nugget in the world was at the Golden Nugget Hotel (of course). There was a real roller coaster on top of the New York–New York hotel. And if you wanted to see a chunk of the Berlin Wall, you could come to Las Vegas. In this one town, Mrs. McDonald would be able to gather a year's worth of material for *Amazing but True*.

Even Dr. McDonald was fascinated, especially when he drove past the National Atomic Testing Museum on East Flamingo Road. He had been thinking about his book idea, and this would be a great place to do research.

"This town is cool!" Coke said. "Can we live here?"

"For two nights you can," said Dr. McDonald as he

pulled into the Mirage, one of the larger hotels on the Strip. He handed the car keys to the valet and went to check in at the front desk.

All the hotels in Las Vegas are also casinos, and the twins had never been in one before. Once they walked through the front door, there were hundreds of slot machines all over, clinking and buzzing and flashing to attract customers.

"Can we try one?" Coke asked his parents. "It says they're only a dollar."

"Kids aren't allowed to gamble," Dr. McDonald told him. "You have to be eighteen before you can throw your money away."

It was getting late, so rather than go out and search for a place to eat, their parents decided to stay in the hotel. There are twelve—yes *twelve*—restaurants in the Mirage. Mrs. McDonald chose Paradise Café, which specialized in "exotic drinks and light fare." Not too fancy.

During dinner, Dr. McDonald kept looking at his watch as if he had to go somewhere. The waiter brought the check a few minutes before eight o'clock.

"Follow me," their father abruptly told the twins. "I want to show you something."

The whole family followed him out to the front of the hotel, where a crowd was forming.

"What's going on?" Pep asked.

"You'll see," her father replied.

The crowd had gathered around a big mountain of rocks. Well, fake rocks, anyway. They were probably made of plastic, like just about everything else in Las Vegas.

At precisely eight o'clock, animal noises and eerie jungle music started to play near the rock mountain. Then, a few wispy puffs of smoke appeared to come out of the top of it.

"I'm scared, Mommy!" a little girl said, clutching her mother's leg.

But things were about to get scarier. As the native drumming became more intense, pink, yellow, and orange flames shot high out of the top of the mountain.

Suddenly, two pirates—or guys dressed like pirates, anyway—came running over.

"Gangway, landlubbers!" shouted the first pirate.

"Ahoy there!" shouted the second one. "Which of you lads or lassies is going to walk the plank?

"Ha-ha!" laughed Mrs. McDonald. "They must have come over from the pirate show at Treasure Island down the street."

The pirates stalked the crowd, looking everybody over. Rows of torches in the water around the mountain of rocks started flaming up.

"Well, shiver me timbers!" said the first pirate as he approached Coke. "*Here's* the bilge-sucking hornswoggler we was lookin' fer!"

"Blimey!" the other pirate said as he came over. "Ye scurvy dog! Let's flog him on the poop deck, matey!"

"I got me a better idea," said the first pirate. "Let's send him to Davy Jones' Locker!"

With that, they grabbed Coke and hoisted him over their shoulders.

"Hey, knock it off," Coke protested.

"Stop!" Pep shouted. "Leave my brother alone!"

"Relax, honey," said Mrs. McDonald. "It's all part of the show."

"Dead men tell no tales," one of the pirates said as they carried Coke up the mountain of rocks. As they did, Coke got a close look at their faces.

"Bowler dudes!" he exclaimed.

"Right you *arrrr*!" cracked the mustachioed bowler dude. "Long time no see!"

"Let me go!" Coke shouted, struggling to get free.

"Yo ho ho!" shouted the first pirate. "We're gonna throw this scalawag into the volcano!"

🦌

See? I *told* you that Coke was going to get thrown into a volcano! But you didn't believe me. Well, I can hardly blame you after that business with the snakes back in chapter 13. But let's continue. . . .

One of the bowler dude pirates grabbed Coke's arms and the other one took his legs. They began swinging him back and forth. The crowd began clapping rhythmically.

"No! Don't!" Coke yelled.

"One . . . two . . . three . . ."

With that, they tossed Coke into the volcano.

Fortunately, the volcano was a fake. If the bowler dudes had thrown him into a *real* volcano, Coke would have crashed into the rocks or been burned alive by molten hot lava. Inside this volcano was an intricate computer system that produced incredibly realistic smoke, light, and sound effects.

Oh, and there were two other things inside the volcano.

Bones and Mya.

When Coke came flying over the edge, they caught him before he could hit the bottom.

"You're safe," Mya said. "It's not a real volcano. They're just playing with your head."

"What are *you* doing here?" Coke asked.

"No time to talk now," Bones said. "We'll come by

your room tomorrow so we can swap information."

"Get back out there," Mya told him. "You're part of the show."

Coke climbed out of the volcano to the applause of the crowd. The bowler dude pirates had already dashed away, cackling and giggling like the idiots they are. The flaming torches flared in time with the music, and then they were extinguished as the volcano show came to an end.

"You have to admit, that was cool," Dr. McDonald said as the crowd began to disperse.

"I love Vegas!" said Mrs. McDonald as they walked back to their rooms. "Where else in the world do they put on a free volcano show every night?"

"What was *that* all about?" Pep asked her brother.

"Tell you later," he whispered.

🦌

"We have a big day planned," Mrs. McDonald announced when she woke the twins up the next morning. "I want to go to the Mob Museum, see the fountains at the Bellagio, that fake Eiffel Tower—"

"And I can't wait to go to the National Atomic Testing Museum," said Dr. McDonald.

The two of them were as giddy as schoolchildren.

"We don't want to go," Coke announced.

"What do you mean you don't want to go?" asked Mrs. McDonald, irritated. "We're a family."

"You told us that since we turned thirteen, we were old enough to do things on our own," Pep said.

"Yeah, maybe we want to do different stuff than you do," Coke said.

The truth was, the twins didn't want to do *anything*. Those crazy bowler dudes were out there on the Strip somewhere. Maybe Dr. Warsaw and John Pain were lurking around too. Coke figured it would be safer if he and Pep stayed in the hotel room. Besides, Mya and Bones had promised to come by.

"What is it that *you* kids want to do?" asked Dr. McDonald.

"We want to watch TV," Coke said.

"So let me get this straight," said Dr. McDonald. "Instead of going out and having fun at all these cool Las Vegas sights, you'd rather sit in a hotel room and watch TV?"

Coke and Pep nodded.

"You're going to miss all the fun," said their mother.

"We've had a lot of fun," Pep said. "We just want to relax today. Maybe we'll take a swim in the pool."

"Suit yourselves," Dr. McDonald said with a sigh. "But your mother and I are going out. Come on, Bridge."

They gave the twins money for breakfast and left,

shaking their heads and wondering—like all parents—what was wrong with the younger generation.

A half hour later, there was a soft knock at the hotel room door.

"Room service," somebody said on the other side.

"We didn't order any room service," Pep replied.

"It's not room service, you dope!" Coke said. "It's *them*!"

He opened the door and Mya and Bones were standing there, in Mirage uniforms. Bones was pushing a rolling cart filled with eggs, toast, orange juice, and sliced melon.

"Breakfast is served!" Mya announced.

As the twins chowed down, Mya and Bones gave them an update on what was going on.

"It's good you didn't go outside today," Mya told them. "Those bowler dudes are checked in at Treasure Island right up the street, for one night only."

"Remember Mrs. Higgins, your so-called health teacher?" asked Bones. "She's working as a psychic healer in Sedona, Arizona."

"We know," Pep said. "We saw her. She didn't try to hurt us at all. She says she's no longer working for Dr. Warsaw."

"Can she be trusted?" asked Coke.

"Maybe," Bones said. "She's no longer in love with

him. We believe she's come to her senses."

"What about John Pain?" asked Pep.

"His whereabouts are unknown."

"And Dr. Warsaw?"

"He was checked into an insane asylum in Arizona, but he escaped," said Mya. "We understand he has acquired enough uranium to build a briefcase bomb, but hasn't assembled it yet. We don't know what his intentions are."

Pep pulled out her notepad with the four ciphers written in it.

"If only we could figure out how those clues tie together," she said. "I'll bet it would lead us to him."

Bones and Mya looked at the notepad, but it made no more sense to them than it did to Pep.

"We need to be on high alert now," Mya said. "We feel that Dr. Warsaw may try to set off his bomb very soon, possibly in the next few days."

"We'll be *home* in a few days," Coke said. "We're only about five hundred miles from San Francisco now."

The thought of Dr. Warsaw confronting them in their home made Coke visibly upset. It was obvious to Bones and Mya that he was not the same confident, cocky boy they had met five weeks earlier.

"It will all be over soon," Bones said, putting an arm

on Coke's shoulder. "We promise you. Stay strong. You'll need each other now more than ever. Here, we brought you a little present."

He pulled a "Welcome to Las Vegas" Frisbee out of his bag.

"A Frisbee grenade?" Coke asked, brightening.

"No, it doesn't explode or anything like that," Mya replied.

"Does it decompose and give off a noxious gas that poisons the person who catches it?" Coke asked hopefully. "That would be cool."

"No."

"Maybe it emits an ear-piercing shriek that blows out their eardrums?" asked Coke.

"No, you just throw it back and forth," Bones explained, "for *fun*."

"Gee, thanks," Pep said, taking the Frisbee.

Mya and Bones left. Coke flipped on the TV, but there was nothing good on. He tried to read a magazine, but his mind kept wandering. He couldn't get Dr. Warsaw, John Pain, and those crazy bowler dudes out of his head.

"I'm going stir-crazy in this room," he finally said to his sister. Let's go someplace."

"You heard what Mya said," Pep told him. "The bowler dudes are right down the street. As soon as we set foot outside this hotel, they'll be all over us."

"Then let's go swim in the hotel pool."

"Well, okay . . ."

They put on their bathing suits and took the elevator down to the lobby, following the POOL signs. Lining the hallway, as everywhere else, were dozens of slot machines.

"Hey, let's try one," Coke said. "I have a dollar."

"You heard what Dad said," Pep told him. "Kids aren't allowed to gamble. It's against the law."

"Dad will never know," Coke replied, looking both ways and fishing a dollar bill out of his pocket. "Come on, let's do it."

"What if you win?" Pep said. "You know, if you hit the jackpot, lights start flashing and bells start ringing. I've seen it in movies. If you hit the jackpot, we'll be in all kinds of trouble."

"What are the chances of *that* happening?" Coke told his sister. "They program these things so you'll *lose*. That's how casinos make money. Everybody knows that."

"Well, if you're so sure you're gonna lose," Pep asked, throwing her hands up, "why do it in the first place? You're just throwing your money away. Just like Dad said."

"It'll be fun!"

Coke looked around to make sure nobody was watching, and then slipped his dollar into the nearest slot machine.

"Go ahead," he said. "Give it a pull. What are they gonna do, throw us in jail?"

Pep sighed, and pulled the lever.

The screen of the slot machine had four squares on it. They spun vertically for a few seconds, and then stopped. Whether you won or lost depended on how many of the squares matched up.

When the squares stopped spinning, this is what was on the screen. . . .

"Isn't it supposed to be pictures of cherries and fruit and stuff like that?" Pep asked.

She looked at the screens of the slot machines on

either side. None of them had numbers.

No coins slid out on the tray at the bottom, but a few seconds later, a card slid out. It was the size of a business card. In fact, it *was* a business card. Pep gasped when she saw what was printed on it. . . .

DR. HERMAN WARSAW

INVENTOR/CONSULTANT/GENIUS

On the back of the card, handwritten in pencil, were five words. . . .

This is the last one

Go to Google Maps (http://maps.google.com).

Click Get Directions.

In the A box, type Las Vegas NV.

In the B box, type Baker CA.

Click Get Directions.

"That means 8980 is a cipher!" Pep shouted. "And it's the *last* one!"

The twins never made it to the pool. They went back to the room to try to figure out what it all meant.

CIPHER #1: MAY 28, 1937, VOLKSWAGEN IS FOUNDED

CIPHER #2: 49:08. 28:40.5

CIPHER #3: FIREWEED
CIPHER #4: BULLARD
CIPHER #5: 8980

It still didn't make sense. But very soon, it would.

Chapter 21
FUN
IN THE
SUN

"You kids missed all the *fun!*" Mrs. McDonald gushed when she got back to the hotel room.

She and Dr. McDonald proceeded to regale Coke and Pep with stories of their adventures visiting many of the oddball museums and attractions Las Vegas had to offer. Her only regret, she said, was that the Liberace Museum had closed several years earlier.

"So what did you two do while we were out?" asked Dr. McDonald.

"Nothing."

Everybody got a good night's sleep, and after

checking out of the hotel in the morning, the family stuffed themselves at one of the many all-you-can-eat breakfast buffets found on the Strip.

Mrs. McDonald started grabbing snacks to munch on in the car, but the rest of the family convinced her that would be unethical—if not illegal—so she put everything back.

"It's all-you-can-*eat*, Mom," Pep scolded her. "Not all-you-can-stuff-in-your-purse."

Everybody had gorged themselves. It was hard to imagine being hungry after a Las Vegas buffet.

"I don't want to eat again for the rest of my life," Coke said, rubbing his belly.

There are only a few roads heading west out of Las Vegas. Dr. McDonald pulled the Ferrari onto I-15, also known as the Mojave Freeway. In just twenty minutes, the bright lights and glitz of Las Vegas were completely gone and the hot, flat, wide-open spaces of arid Nevada were back. One couldn't help but wonder why human beings had chosen to build a strange playground in the middle of the desert for people to lose their money on slot machines and roulette wheels.

"I have an announcement to make," Dr. McDonald

said shortly after leaving the city limits of Las Vegas.

"Uh-oh," thought both twins. When their father had an announcement to make, it was usually not good news.

"I slept on it," their father continued, "and after going to the Atomic Testing Museum yesterday, I've decided *not* to write that Trinity novel we talked about."

"Why not, Dad?" Pep asked. "That would have been a cool story."

"There are dozens of books about the first atomic test," he explained. "The world doesn't need another one. I want to write something *totally* original."

"Dad, you should write a novel about a guy who can't come up with an idea for a novel to write," Coke suggested.

"It's been done."

"So what are you going to write about, Dad?" Pep asked.

"I don't know," Dr. McDonald replied. "I'll come up with something."

Pep opened her notepad and turned to the page with the five ciphers they had received. She focused on the fifth one. It would be the last one, according to Dr. Warsaw's card.

8980

Numbers were harder to figure out than letters, Pep always found. And four digits didn't give her much to work with. It was obviously a very short message. The Internet wasn't much help. Pep borrowed her mother's laptop and searched for "8980," but all that came up were a bunch of street addresses and model numbers for various products.

After staring at her notepad for a long time, Pep closed it with a sigh. She could work on it again later.

Everyone had settled in for a long drive, but just an hour and a half after leaving Las Vegas, this sign appeared at the side of the road. . . .

As if on cue, the whole family spontaneously burst into that old song—*"Cal-i-forn-ia here I come, right back where I started from . . ."*

Everyone stopped right there, because nobody knew the next line of the song.

"Woo-hoo!" Coke shouted. "We're home, baby!"

Well, not exactly *home*. California is a big, *long* state. If you were to drive from the top to the bottom, it would be about eight hundred miles.

However, if they kept driving without a stop, the McDonalds could be home that very same day. It's only about three hours from the state line to Los Angeles, and after that it's a five-hour straight shot up I-5 to San Francisco. But just knowing that they were finally back in the state of California again made everyone *feel* like they were home.

When you think of Southern California, you probably think of the glamour of Los Angeles—beautiful movie stars, spectacular mansions, swimming pools, and crowded freeways. But here, right near the Nevada border, there was none of that. This part of California is desert, and some of the most unforgiving desolation in the world. If not for the water and electricity supplied by Hoover Dam, parts of Southern California would be virtually uninhabitable.

Mrs. McDonald dropped her Nevada guidebook in the trash. She didn't have one for California. Who buys a guidebook to their own state? She did, however, open her laptop so she could go on the internet and see if the family would be passing by anything she could use in *Amazing but True*.

"Hey, guess what?" she said. "The world's largest thermometer is in Baker, California!"

Dr. McDonald rolled his eyes.

"Bridge," he said delicately, "yesterday we went to the Houdini Museum, the Mob Museum, and the fake Statue of Liberty. How about we take a break today? Is it *really* crucially important for you to see the world's largest thermometer?"

"Yes!"

Dr. McDonald gritted his teeth and sighed. Once again, he knew he was going to be the one to give in. He had to. It was *Amazing but True* that paid for the whole vacation. That silly website earned a ridiculous amount of money. It was only fair for Mrs. McDonald to decide where they would go on the trip. This was another reason why he wanted to write a novel. If he could get on the bestseller list, he would be a more equal partner when it came to making these kinds of decisions.

"Oh, come on, Ben," Mrs. McDonald said, more sweetly. "The world's largest thermometer is right on our way. We don't even have to get off the road."

That was true. Less than 50 miles from the California state line, they reached the little town of Baker, punctuated by gas stations and fast food joints.

"There it is!" Pep shouted, pointing at the distant structure sticking up out of the ground.

The world's largest thermometer is hard to miss. You can see it for miles around.

"Pull over, Ben!" Mrs. McDonald suddenly shouted. The thermometer was still several blocks away.

"What? Did I hit something?" Dr. McDonald yelled as he slammed on the brakes and swerved off the road into a parking lot.

He hadn't hit anything. But he had almost driven right past Baker, California's, *other* claim to fame, the Alien Fresh Jerky store!

"We've *got* to stop here," said Mrs. McDonald.

It was irresistible. On the outside of Alien Fresh Jerky was a fake flying saucer and an alien sitting on top of a sign and waving a cowboy hat. On the inside was a mechanical alien fortune-teller, alien mugs, refrigerator magnets, and similar knickknacks. That, and "the best jerky in the universe," of course.

"I wonder if Moe, Larry, and Curly have been here," Pep whispered to her brother.

"They probably *own* the joint," Coke whispered back.

Nobody was hungry after their big breakfast, but Mrs. McDonald bought a few strips of beef, gator, and turkey jerky for souvenirs. She took some notes and photos for *Amazing but True*, and then it was back in the Ferrari to drive to the giant thermometer, just past some palm trees down the road.

"So this is it, eh?" asked Dr. McDonald as he got out of the car.

The world's largest thermometer was, to be honest, a bit of a disappointment. Admittedly, it *is* large—134 feet tall and 76,812 pounds. But it isn't really a working thermometer. It's just a sign made to *look like* a thermometer.

"Man, it's hot out here," Pep said, wiping her forehead.

"Yeah," Coke replied, "too bad there isn't a thermometer around so we can know the temperature."

"Very funny," Mrs. McDonald said as she dutifully took photos and notes. The fans of *Amazing but True* would appreciate the world's largest thermometer, even if it wasn't a working thermometer.

Dr. McDonald noticed the words at the bottom of the thermometer, and they prompted him to pull out his road atlas.

"Hey, guys," he said. "Did you know that Death Valley is less than two hours from here?"

"So?" Pep asked.

"We should go there," said her father.

"What's at Death Valley, Ben?" asked Mrs. McDonald. "Isn't it a bunch of nothing?"

"It's supposed to be *amazing*," said Dr. McDonald. "There's lots of wildlife, and it's the lowest elevation in the United States.

Parts of it are actually *below* sea level."

Death Valley didn't sound particularly exciting to Mrs. McDonald. What interested her were wacky museums, halls of fame, and tacky tourist traps. As far as the kids were concerned, just the name "Death Valley" gave them the creeps.

"Why do you want to go to Death Valley?" Coke asked his father. "Couldn't we get stranded in the desert and die there? Isn't that why it's called Death Valley in the first place?"

"You watch too many movies," his father said. "There's a Death Valley National Park there. How dangerous could it be if they have a national park?"

"Well, you indulged *me*, Ben," said Mrs. McDonald, putting her arm around him. "If you want to take a little spontaneous detour to Death Valley, I say let's do it."

"Oh man," Coke whined. "We've been on the road for more than five *weeks* now. I just want to get *home*!"

"Me too," agreed Pep.

"Look, we've come this far," Dr. McDonald told the twins. "Death Valley could end up to be the highlight of the whole trip. Come on, where's your sense of adventure?"

Go to Google Maps
(http://maps.google.com).

Click Get Directions.

In the A box, type
Baker CA.

In the B box, type
Death Valley State Park
CA.

Click Get Directions.

Route 127 starts in Baker and goes north over 100 miles to Death Valley. It's also called Death Valley Road. A mile and a half into the drive, they passed little Baker Airport on the left. After that it was just desert as far as the eye could see.

The Mojave, to be specific. Ten thousand years ago, there used to be a huge lake there. When the water evaporated, it left miles of salt flats, low-lying shrubs, and a few hearty snakes, spiders, and wildlife that could survive one of the harshest environments on earth.

"We're lucky we have air-conditioning," Pep said.

Coke cracked his window open a few inches, and hot air rushed into the car. He quickly closed the window again.

The climate of Death Valley is the result of being below sea level and surrounded by mountains. Hot, dry air masses get trapped in the valley and sit there. The highest temperature *ever* recorded was right in Death Valley, on July 10, 1913, when it reached 134 degrees Fahrenheit. That is *hot*. It's not at all unusual for the temperature to get into the 120-degree range during the summer.

They say that bighorn sheep, coyotes, bobcats, and mountain lions roam the area, but the McDonalds didn't see any as they drove toward Death Valley. All they saw were windswept sand dunes, a few dilapidated wooden shacks, and the occasional rusted-out, abandoned car.

And yet, there was something *beautiful* about Death Valley. It was almost like visiting another planet.

"I'm glad we decided to come here," Dr. McDonald said. "Think of it. There probably isn't another human being for miles around. This is what *all* of North America used to look like just a few hundred years ago, guys. No advanced civilization. No fast food joints or ugly strip malls. Just nature. And someday, after our species is extinct, this is what America will look like again."

"You're totally bumming me out, Dad," Coke said.

"I'd sure hate to get stuck here," said Pep.

Seconds after she said that, there was a crunching sound from below, followed by a series of quick *bang*s.

"Uh-oh," said Dr. McDonald.

The car rolled to a stop, the engine went silent, and the air-conditioning shut down. Almost instantly, the temperature inside the car jumped twenty degrees. There was the unmistakable smell of something burning.

"What's the matter, Ben?" asked Mrs. McDonald.

Dr. McDonald didn't reply. He got out of the car and raised the hood. The rest of the family went out to peer at the engine, too.

"Can you fix it, Dad?" Pep asked.

"I don't know anything about cars," her father replied.

"Then why did you pick up the hood, Dad?" Coke asked, knowing he wasn't going to get an answer.

Mrs. McDonald took out her cell phone and tried to call for help, but there was no cell service this far away from a town. The other three tried their phones, with the same result.

"Somebody will come along any minute," Mrs. McDonald said hopefully. "Everything is going to be fine."

"It's so *hot* out here," Pep groaned, fanning herself. "I can't take it."

"Maybe I should take a walk up the road and see if there's a gas station or something," Dr. McDonald mused.

"It's the *desert*, Ben," Mrs. McDonald told him. "There hasn't been a gas station for *miles*. You might *die* out there in this heat."

"We might die right *here* in this heat too," Coke pointed out.

"We'll just have to wait," his mother said.

So they waited. There was no shade nearby and the car was too hot to sit in, so the family sat on the ground next to the car, using it as a shield to partly block the sun. There was nothing else they could do.

"Maybe you kids want to throw your Frisbee around while we're waiting for help?" Mrs. McDonald suggested.

Pep had become increasingly adept at throwing a Frisbee over the last five weeks, and had taken to carrying one with her wherever she went.

"It's too hot," she replied.

A slight breeze came along, which in ordinary

circumstances would have cooled things off. But it was hot air, and that just made it worse. Mrs. McDonald took off her earrings because they had become so hot that they hurt her ears. Coke took off his T-shirt and tied it around his head. None of the McDonalds had thought to put on sunscreen that morning. They didn't know they would be taking this detour to Death Valley.

"Mom, do we have any water?" Pep asked. "I'm so thirsty."

"We should have bought some while we were in Baker," her mother replied.

"The car's radiator must have water in it," Coke pointed out. "If we had to, we could drink that."

"I'm sure that water isn't good for you," his father said.

"Neither are dehydration and heat stroke," Coke said. "Do we have anything to eat? Food has water in it."

"The only thing I have is that jerky I bought," said Mrs. McDonald.

"Oh, *great*," Coke said. "We're stuck in the desert with no water, and our only food was specifically made by removing the moisture from it."

"I don't like jerky anyway," Pep said.

"Beggars can't be choosers," said Mrs. McDonald,

annoyed. "If you recall, I was *going* to stuff my purse with snacks at the all-you-can-eat buffet this morning. If you hadn't treated me like I was a common criminal, we would have some food now."

"I'd give anything for one of those breakfast pastries," Pep said.

"I'm burning up," Coke complained, fanning himself. "I never felt so hot in my life."

Dr. McDonald didn't feel like talking. He got up and walked a few yards off the road, looking at the cracked, dry earth. He was surprised to see a few flowers that had somehow managed to survive the desert. But he also saw the bleached white skull of some large animal, maybe a goat. He didn't tell the rest of the family about it. He didn't want to alarm them.

"What happens if nobody comes to rescue us?" Pep asked after some time had passed.

"Somebody will come," his father said. "Think positive."

"But what happens if they *don't*?" Pep persisted.

"We'll die," Coke told his sister. "That's what happens if nobody comes to rescue us. You can't survive long in this environment without water."

"We're *not* going to die!" Mrs. McDonald insisted hoarsely. "Don't talk like that!"

An hour had passed. Their four throats were dry. Dr. McDonald kept looking up and down the road hopefully, but there were no cars in either direction. High overhead, a few birds were circling ominously.

"Are those vultures?" Pep asked.

"Yeah," Coke told her. "They're scavengers. They wait for animals to get sick and die. Then they come down and eat everything but the bones."

"Stop talking like that!" said Mrs. McDonald. "They're not even vultures. They're hawks."

Another hour passed. The sun was lower, but the heat was unrelenting. It would be several hours before the sun went down, providing some relief. Everyone was starting to feel weak and tired, common signs of dehydration.

"My tongue feels like a piece of wood in my mouth," Pep said. "I can barely swallow."

Just speaking required effort, and it was important to conserve energy. But unrelenting quiet can be oppressive too. Coke in particular felt a need to break the silence.

"The amazing thing is that this is one of the lowest spots in North America," he informed the rest of the family, "but just seventy-six miles from here is Mount Whitney, the highest elevation in the contiguous United States."

"Nobody cares," Pep muttered.

"Y'know," Coke persisted, "I read in a magazine article that part of the original *Star Wars* movie was filmed in Death Valley. Remember that scene with Luke Skywalker—"

"Shut up!" the others shouted.

As everyone became increasingly uncomfortable and frustrated, tempers were growing short.

"This is all *your* fault, Ben," Mrs. McDonald said.

"What did *I* do?" Dr. McDonald replied.

"I *told* you to get a *practical* car. A Ferrari is *not* a practical car."

"*Any* car could have broken down out here, Bridge! Don't blame it on the Ferrari."

"I'm not blaming it on the Ferrari, Ben. I'm blaming it on your judgment. You bought the stupid car, and it was your stupid idea to come to Death Valley in the first place. The rest of us wanted to drive straight home."

"Don't call me stupid."

"I didn't say *you* were stupid. I said the car was

stupid, and it was a stupid idea to come here."

"Fighting doesn't solve anything, you guys," Coke told his parents. He had never seen them fight like that.

"Are you going to get divorced?" Pep asked.

"You can't get divorced if you're dead," Coke said.

"We're not going to die!" both parents shouted.

In the back of his mind, Coke wondered if perhaps someone had sabotaged the Ferrari. When they were at the Grand Canyon, he remembered, somebody had broken in and written that cipher in Pep's notepad. Maybe they also had tampered with the engine in some way that would cause a breakdown a few hundred miles down the road. There was no way of knowing.

It didn't matter at this point, anyway. All that mattered was that they were stuck in Death Valley and if somebody didn't come soon, it would be all over.

"I'm *so* thirsty," Pep groaned. "Now I know how the Donner Party felt."

The Donner Party didn't die from thirst, but everybody was too tired to argue the point.

"I've heard of people who were so thirsty that they drank urine to survive," Coke said. "It's mostly water."

"That's disgusting," Pep muttered. "I'm not drinking your pee."

"You don't have to drink *my* pee. You can drink your *own* pee."

"I'm not drinking *anybody's* pee!"

"I'm so sleepy," Mrs. McDonald said. "I'm going to take a nap."

"Don't do that, Bridge," Dr. McDonald told her. "If you go to sleep you may never wake up."

"I don't *want* to wake up," she replied wearily. "I just want to sleep."

As the afternoon wore on, the heat sapped what little strength was left in the McDonalds. They say Death Valley is so hot in the summer that you can fry an egg on a rock. That is, of course, if you had an egg. The McDonalds had nothing to eat, nothing to drink, and nowhere to go. A sense of gloom came over the family. Mrs. McDonald closed her eyes.

"I can't believe it," Pep mumbled. "After everything that's happened to us on our trip, *this* is how we're going to die."

"What do you mean?" her father asked. "What *else* happened to you on the trip?"

"What else?" Coke said, almost in a whisper now because his throat was so dry. "Remember when we went to that french fry demonstration at the first McDonald's in Illinois?"

"Yeah."

"That kid who looked like Archie from the comics tried to kill us by throwing us into boiling oil."

His father looked at him, incredulous.

"And remember the time we went to that amusement park in Ohio?" asked Pep.

"Yeah."

"We were kidnapped on a roller coaster, tied up in a Mister Softee truck, and nearly frozen to death in ice cream."

"We were trapped in a recording studio at the Rock and Roll Hall of Fame and forced to listen to heavy metal music so loud our heads almost exploded," Coke told his father.

"We were kidnapped at the Museum of American History," recalled Pep, "and locked in vapor cabinets in Hot Springs, Arkansas."

"In Dallas, I was run over by two guys on motorcycles at the exact spot where President Kennedy was shot," Coke said.

"Our bowling shoes were poisoned at the Bowling Hall of Fame," said Pep, "and we were swarmed by flying bats under that bridge in Austin, Texas . . ."

"You mean to tell me that all those things actually *happened* to you?" Dr. McDonald asked. "Are you sure you're not hallucinating from the heat?"

"We're sure," Coke replied. "We've been trying to

tell you about this stuff the whole trip. You wouldn't believe us."

"I thought you were just joking."

"It all happened, Dad," Pep said, "and lots more stuff happened, too. I'm too tired to go into it all."

"Wow," Dr. McDonald said. "You're blowing my mind. Why did those people do all those horrible things to you?"

"It's a long story," Coke said. "It doesn't matter now, Dad. It's all over."

Dr. McDonald sobbed, putting an arm around each of his children.

"I'm a terrible father," he said.

"No, Dad, you're great," Pep said.

"You're the best father in the world," Coke assured him.

"I just want you kids to know that your mother and I *really* tried to make this a special family vacation for you," Dr. McDonald told them. "All I can say is I'm sorry. And I'm sorry I didn't believe you when you told us about all those things. I love you kids more than anything in the world."

"We love you, too, Dad," the twins replied, sobbing along with their father.

Having made their peace with each other, one by one the McDonalds dropped off to sleep, leaning against the car and each other.

They would have stayed asleep, too, if not for the sound of an engine in the distance.

"What's that?" Dr. McDonald asked, shaking himself awake and struggling to his feet. "Is that a car?"

Coke and Pep stood up, too. There was *something* moving in the distance. But the view was fuzzy from the heat on the horizon.

"It may be a mirage," Coke said. "That's what happens when people get stranded in the desert without water. They start seeing things that aren't there. It's wishful thinking."

"It *is* a car!" Pep shouted, somehow managing to jump up and down with whatever energy she had left. "We're saved!"

An old blue minivan came into view and rolled to a stop next to them. There were peace signs painted on the side. The driver rolled down the window.

It was Mrs. Higgins.

Chapter 22

A NEW WOMAN

O f *all* the people in the world who could have driven down this particular desolate road at this particular moment in time, why did it *have* to be Mrs. Audrey Higgins?

She had set the twins' school on fire—while they were in it. She had chased them through The House on the Rock in Wisconsin. She had unleashed an angry mob of baseball fans on them in Illinois, blasted their eardrums at the Rock and Roll Hall of Fame in Ohio, and poisoned their bowling shoes in Texas. She had changed personalities numerous times, and most recently showed up as a kindly psychic named Aurora Moonbeam in Arizona. And now she was the only thing between the McDonald family and death at Death Valley.

"Oh my God!" Mrs. Higgins hollered. "Are you folks okay?"

Coke, Pep, and their father staggered toward the minivan like zombies in a horror movie. They could barely speak. Mrs. McDonald was still sitting on the ground, leaning against the Ferrari. She was too weak to stand.

At first, the twins didn't recognize Mrs. Higgins, who was wearing a sunhat and dark glasses, like any sensible person should while traveling through the desert.

She grabbed a jug of water from her minivan and started filling plastic cups. Coke, Pep, and Dr. McDonald guzzled gratefully and accepted seconds.

"Just let me die here," Mrs. McDonald mumbled, her eyes still closed. "I just want to go to sleep."

Mrs. Higgins poured water on Mrs. McDonald's head and forced her to drink. As a health teacher, she had extensive experience in first aid, and knew exactly what to do in situations of dehydration and heat stroke. Once the water touched her lips, Mrs. McDonald was revived somewhat and drank heartily, like the others.

"Let me pay you," said Dr. McDonald, who was regaining his faculties. "I want to give you some money. . . ."

He fumbled with his wallet, but she pushed it away.

"Don't be silly," Mrs. Higgins told him. "You don't recognize me, do you? We met at the Bauxite Museum in Arkansas."

"Of course!" said Dr. McDonald. "You're the health teacher from school! It is so nice to see you again. What are you doing in this godforsaken place?"

"I'm on my way home, just like you," Mrs. Higgins replied. "I got an email the other day. Construction at the new school is underway and they offered me my old job back."

Coke and Pep looked at each other. They were hanging back, not sure if it would be wise to become involved with Mrs. Higgins again. Her blind love of Dr. Warsaw had caused her to do terrible things. But other times it appeared that she'd changed her ways. You never knew what you were going to get with her.

Dr. McDonald helped his wife to her feet and walked her around the area to get her blood pumping again. That left the twins alone with Mrs. Higgins, who handed each of them a protein bar from her purse. Ravenous, they tore off the wrappers and wolfed them down.

"Hop in!" she said, "I'll give you folks a lift back home."

"Why are you being so nice to us?" Pep asked her. "You tried to kill us over and over again."

"I told you, I changed," Mrs. Higgins replied. "I *mean* it this time. When I finally realized that Dr. Warsaw would never love me, I decided to let go of him. I became a new woman. Even the worst people in the world are capable of changing, you know."

"Even Dr. Warsaw?" Pep asked.

"Yes," she replied. "But I fear that Herman is only going to change for the worse. He is mentally ill."

The twins were still wary about getting into a car with this woman, who had exhibited psychotic behavior herself just days earlier.

"Fine," said Mrs. Higgins cheerfully. "You can stay here if you'd like. The sun will be setting soon, and that will cool things off a bit. But then, of course, that's when the coyotes and mountain lions come out."

Coke and Pep climbed into the car, taking the third row of seats. Mrs. Higgins helped Dr. McDonald transfer their luggage from the Ferrari into the minivan.

As the parents climbed into the second row of seats, Dr. McDonald hesitated.

"What about the Ferrari?" he asked.

"Forget the Ferrari, Ben!" Mrs. McDonald shouted

hoarsely. "We can deal with it later. Let's get out of here."

Mrs. Higgins started up the minivan and turned the air-conditioning up full blast. As the cool air blew over them, the McDonalds gave a collective sigh of relief.

"We can't thank you enough," Mrs. McDonald said. "You saved our lives."

"I can't believe you folks came to Death Valley with no water and no food," Mrs. Higgins said. "And it looks like you got a nasty sunburn there, Dr. McDonald. What were you thinking?"

"I wasn't," he replied.

Go to Google Maps (http://maps.google.com).

Click Get Directions.

In the A box, type Death Valley CA.

In the B box, type San Francisco CA.

Click Get Directions.

Chapter 23

THE FINAL CHAPTER

The drive from Death Valley to San Francisco was one of the longest stretches of the whole trip. Several national forests sit right in the middle, so it's necessary to drive a big loop around them. They would pass through Red Rock Canyon State Park and Bakersfield before connecting up with I-5, which goes almost directly to San Francisco. The trip would be over 500 miles.

Dr. McDonald was exhausted, but fortunately he didn't have to do the driving. Mrs. Higgins was happy to chauffeur, and the McDonalds insisted on paying for gas and tolls. One by one the family dropped off to sleep. It had been a long, hard day.

Coke, Pep, and their parents slept the whole night until they were jostled awake at sunrise when the minivan was bumping over the hills and streets of San Francisco. As they drove down the Embarcadero on the waterfront, they caught their first familiar glimpse of the Golden Gate Bridge, six miles away. It is considered to be one of the most beautiful bridges in the world.

"We're almost home!" Pep said, stretching.

"Did you sleep well?" Mrs. Higgins asked. "You folks were *out*."

"Like a baby," said Dr. McDonald.

Mrs. McDonald noticed a California guidebook on

the floor between the two front seats.

"May I look at this?" she asked.

"Of course," Mrs. Higgins replied.

"We're not stopping *anywhere*, Bridge," said Dr. McDonald sternly. "Don't even *think* about it. No more museums. No more halls of fame. No more roadside tourist traps. We're going straight home now."

"I just want to see what it says about the Golden Gate," said Mrs. McDonald. "I've driven over this bridge so many times, but I really don't know much about it."

In fact, the McDonalds had driven over the Golden Gate Bridge at the start of their trip five weeks earlier. Mrs. McDonald leafed through the guidebook until she found the section about the bridge.

"Let's see. It says here that the Golden Gate opened on May 28, 1937 . . ."

"Nobody cares, Mom," Pep shouted from the back.

"Wait a minute," Coke said to his sister. "Did she say May 28, 1937? Open your notepad!"

Pep pulled out her notepad and flipped to the page where she had written all the ciphers.

"That's the first cipher!" Pep whispered excitedly to her brother. "Maybe May 28, 1937, doesn't have anything to do with Volkswagen at all! Maybe it's just a coincidence that the company started the same day the Golden Gate Bridge opened!"

"What else does that guidebook say about the bridge, Mom?" Coke asked.

"Let me see . . . ," Mrs. McDonald said. "Oh, this is interesting. It tells the exact longitude and latitude for the bridge. It's north 37 degrees, 49 minutes, and 8 seconds. And it's west 122 degrees, 28 minutes, and 40.5 seconds."

"That *is* interesting," said Mrs. Higgins.

Coke and Pep looked at each other. Then they looked at the notepad.

"The second cipher!" Pep said. "The minutes and seconds didn't refer to a *time*! They referred to a *location*! The location of the Golden Gate Bridge!"

"Listen to this," Mrs. McDonald went on. "It says here that they are constantly repainting the bridge. The paint is supplied by Sherwin Williams."

"I used their paint on the garage last year," Dr. McDonald said. "Does it mention what color they use? The bridge isn't gold. It's more like a reddish orange."

"It says the color code is SW 6328," said Mrs. McDonald. "It's called 'Fireweed.'"

The twins just about jumped out of their seats.

"Fireweed?!"

"That's what it says."

"That's the third cipher!" Pep whispered to her

brother. "Fireweed isn't the plant! It's the color of the Golden Gate Bridge!"

"Here's something I bet you don't know," said Mrs. McDonald. "The hardhat was invented when they were building the bridge."

"Hardhat?" asked Mrs. Higgins. "You mean those yellow helmets construction workers wear?"

"Yeah," Mrs. McDonald said. "It says here that an American soldier came home after World War One and he designed a hardhat for miners based on the helmet he wore in the army. The guys who worked on bridges back then had stuff falling on them all the time, so this soldier designed a helmet just for them. It was used for the first time when they were building the Golden Gate Bridge."

"What was the guy's name?" Coke asked.

"E. W. Bullard," his mother replied.

"Bullard?!"

"That's the fourth cipher!" Pep whispered.

"Mom, does it say anything about the number 8980?" Coke asked.

Mrs. McDonald scanned the guidebook.

"Oh yeah," she said. "That's how long the bridge is.

Eight thousand, nine hundred and eighty feet."

Both twins slapped their foreheads.

"*All* the ciphers have something to do with the Golden Gate Bridge!" Pep whispered. "How could we have been so blind?"

"It was right under our noses the whole time," Coke whispered. "Something is going to happen on the bridge."

"And it looks like it may be happening right *now*," Pep said, pointing in front of them.

The traffic leading onto the bridge had slowed to a standstill. It appeared as though the police had shut down the bridge in both directions. Drivers were honking their horns in frustration. In the distance, the siren of an ambulance or a fire truck was blaring. Some people had gotten out of their cars to see what was going on up ahead.

"I don't feel good about this," Pep said.

A helicopter was hovering on the side of the bridge. The famous prison island, Alcatraz, could be seen in the distance. In the water, a coast guard boat bobbed up and down. A group of guys in white hazmat suits ran by. Whatever was happening, it was too far in front to see.

"It must be an accident," said Dr. McDonald. "We could be stuck here for hours."

The twins were not about to wait around.

"Let's go!" Pep said as she grabbed her Frisbee and climbed over her father to scamper out the side door of the minivan. Coke was right behind her on the other side.

"Where are you kids going?" Dr. McDonald shouted after them. "Come back here! It's not your business."

"Oh, yes it is," Coke said as he ran after his sister.

The grown-ups had no choice. All three of them took off their seat belts and got out of the car. Mrs. Higgins was in the lead, but the twins had run way ahead.

The Golden Gate Bridge is a little less than two miles long. It's a suspension bridge, which means the roadway is suspended from wire cables that curve gracefully over the tall towers and are anchored at both ends. To hold up the Golden Gate when it was built in the 1930s, the designers used 80,000 *miles* of cable.

None of the cars on the bridge were moving. Coke and Pep dashed around a few of them and then scaled the four-foot fence that separates the roadway from the pedestrian walkway alongside it. The walkway is about ten feet wide, and it was jammed with people who were walking or bicycling over the bridge.

"Excuse us!" Pep shouted as she weaved and elbowed her way through the crowd.

As the twins got closer to the middle of the bridge, they could see a man in a rumpled brown business suit and carrying a briefcase who had climbed up the main cable at its lowest point. He was standing on the cable, about twenty feet above the roadway. Several policemen and others were trying to talk him down.

"We're not here to hurt you," one of the cops bellowed into a bullhorn. "You might feel like you're alone, but you're not. Let us help you. Tell us your name."

Pep stopped in her tracks when she got close enough to see the man's face.

"It's Dr. Warsaw!"

"He wanted us to come here," Coke said. "That's what all those ciphers were about."

Dr. Warsaw lit a cigarette with one hand and tossed his previous one away. It sailed a long way down into the water. Warsaw had a squinty-eyed smile on his face as he hollered down at the policemen.

"Soon, you'll *all* know my name," he shouted. "Everyone in the *world* will know my name after today."

"Think of your family," the cop hollered, trying to form rapport or find an emotional chord that might touch the deranged man.

"Shut up!" Dr. Warsaw shouted down.

The policeman holding the bullhorn passed it over to another cop, who had more training in suicide prevention.

"You don't want to do this, buddy," the second cop said. "It's two hundred and forty-five feet down. After falling four seconds, you'll be going seventy-five miles per hour when you hit the water. That's gonna hurt. Hurt bad. Tough way to die."

"I said shut up!" Dr. Warsaw shouted down at the cop. "I don't need a freshman physics lesson from *you*!"

"I know you're frustrated, sir," the cop yelled. "But if you do this, you'll be dead on impact, or you'll drown, or you'll die from hypothermia in minutes. The water down there is forty-seven degrees, sir. Best case scenario, you survive and you'll be crippled for life. Do you have a loved one you want to talk this over with? We can get them on the phone."

Dr. Warsaw ignored the cop and started climbing unsteadily up the cable. By that time, Mrs. Higgins had pushed her way through the crowd.

"Do you know that man?" one of the policemen asked her.

"I sure do," she replied, and then she shouted up to Dr. Warsaw. "Don't do it, Herman! Jumping won't solve anything! We'll get you help!"

"I'm not going to kill myself, you idiot!" Dr. Warsaw shouted back. "I'm going to kill *all* of us! There are more than twenty-seven thousand wires inside the cable I'm standing on. Once it snaps, the whole bridge comes down. *Everybody* dies!"

"He's got a bomb!" Coke hollered. "In the briefcase! You've got to stop him!"

The cops, who had been treating this as a "jumper job," suddenly switched into antiterrorism mode. They reached for their guns and pointed them up at Dr. Warsaw.

"Don't shoot him!" Mrs. Higgins begged. "Let me talk to him. *Please!*"

Dr. and Mrs. McDonald, huffing and puffing, finally made their way past all the gawkers. They rushed over and wrapped their arms protectively around Coke and Pep.

"Go ahead, lady," the policeman with the bullhorn

said to Mrs. Higgins. "I'll give you thirty seconds to talk to him before we take him out."

He handed her the bullhorn.

"Herman, don't do this!" Mrs. Higgins shouted. "You're a brilliant scientist and inventor! You don't want to kill all these innocent people!"

"Maybe I *like* killing innocent people!" Dr. Warsaw shouted down at her. "I'm tired of incompetent underlings such as yourself screwing up over and over again. If you want to get a job done right, do it yourself. That's what I say. So I'm doing this myself."

"You could do so much *good* for the world, Herman!" Mrs. Higgins shouted.

"I *tried* to do something good for the world, Audrey. That's what The Genius Files program was all about. But those bratty kids ruined everything. I'm done doing good things for the world."

"We're gonna have to take him out, boys," one of the cops said.

All the other cops cocked the hammers of their pistols.

"But he's not sane!" Mrs. Higgins pleaded. "He's not responsible for his actions!"

"That's not my biggest concern, ma'am," the cop told her. "I'm not going to let some nut destroy this bridge and all the people on it."

The gawkers pushed forward on the roadway. Dozens of people had left their cars and come over to take cell phone pictures of the crazy man on the bridge. There were a few familiar faces in the crowd. John Pain was there. Mya and Bones had come across from the other side of the bridge. Even the bowler dudes had shown up.

"I reckon you're done for, Doc," said John Pain. "It was nice workin' fer ya."

"Go ahead and shoot me," Dr. Warsaw warned the police. "I programmed this briefcase to detonate at the sound of a gunshot. When the bridge comes down, it will be *your* fault."

The cops looked at each other.

"He's bluffing," one of them said. "Ready . . ."

"No, he's not!" screamed Mrs. Higgins. "He's a genius! He is fully capable of building a nuclear device."

"Jump!" shouted the bowler dudes, cackling like the morons they are.

". . . aim . . ."

Dr. Warsaw scanned the crowd below him, a crazed look in his eyes. Those eyes seemed to harden when his gaze fell upon the twins.

"Wait!" Dr. Warsaw shouted. "There are only two people I'm willing to negotiate with. *Those* two!"

He pointed down at Coke and Pep.

"Hold your fire, men!" one of the cops shouted.

Everyone turned to look at the twins. Dr. and Mrs. McDonald held them tighter.

"You know that man?" their mother asked Coke and Pep.

"We sure do," they said simultaneously.

Coke and Pep tore themselves away from their parents' grasp and rushed forward to the edge of the pedestrian walkway. The police cleared a path for them. Pep was leading the way, but her brother grabbed her elbow.

"I want to do this," Coke whispered in his sister's ear.

"Are you sure?" Pep replied. "I mean . . ."

"I'm sure," Coke said. "He's mine. Be my backup. You know what to do."

For a brief instant, Coke and Pep stared into each other's eyes, communicating silently as only twins can.

"Yes! *Those* two spoiled brats!" Dr. Warsaw shouted down. "Coke and Pepsi McDonald. *They* drove me to do this. *They* ruined my life. When this bridge comes down and all you people die, it will be on *their* heads!"

"Why don't you come down here and we'll talk it over?" Coke shouted.

"If you want to talk to me, come up *here*, you little punk!"

Coke took a running leap on the fence and carefully put his foot on the smaller cable that was attached to the round, main cable that held the bridge up. He wrapped his arms and legs around the main cable to make sure he wouldn't fall off.

"Get down from there, Coke!" Dr. McDonald shouted. "Are you crazy?"

Both parents tried to rush forward and grab the twins, but the police held them back.

Coke stood up on the main cable, holding the two wires on either side of it for balance. He was about twenty feet from Dr. Warsaw.

"You're making the biggest mistake of your life," Coke told him. "Don't do this."

"Oh, you and your sister down there are the cause of *all* my troubles," Dr. Warsaw said. "The two of you destroyed my iJolt invention when we first met back in Wisconsin. Remember that? Then, you killed my young protégé, Archie, in Washington. He was the son I never had. He was going to carry on my work when I'm gone."

"He tried to kill *us*!" Coke shouted back, but Dr. Warsaw wasn't in a mood to listen.

"For years I labored to build the perfect robotic

clone of myself," Warsaw continued. "It was my life's work, and you destroyed that, too, at the amusement park in Texas. And worst of all, you killed my dear wife, Judy, your own blood relative, and the only woman I ever loved."

Mrs. McDonald gasped. She never knew what had happened to her sister, Judy, after she disappeared.

"That was an accident!" Pep shouted up from the roadway. "She set our RV on fire!"

"Too many accidents!" Dr. Warsaw hollered angrily. "Don't tell me you kids are innocent. I've chased you two all the way across the country and back. You've evaded me long enough. Remember what I told you? Sometimes you can't fix things. You have to replace them. Well, this is one of those times. They're going to have to replace everything, starting with this bridge. *This* won't be an accident."

He started fiddling with some buttons near the handle of his briefcase.

"Now, Pep!" Coke shouted.

Pep steadied herself, got into position, and took careful aim. Then she reared back and flung her Frisbee up at Dr. Warsaw. It hit him squarely on the back of his right wrist.

"Owww!" he yelled as he released his grasp. "What the—"

He flailed at it, but his reflexes were too slow. The briefcase dropped from his hand and fell over the side of the bridge. Four seconds later, it landed with a splash in the choppy water below.

"Nice toss, Pep!" Coke shouted.

Dr. Warsaw looked around, realizing he had lost his bargaining chip. Below, the cops raised their guns again and trained them on him.

"Now it's just you and me, Warsaw," Coke said.

"I'll kill you with my bare hands if I have to," Dr. Warsaw replied, enraged. "You're no match for me."

"Ready . . . ," shouted the lead policeman, "aim . . ."

Dr. Warsaw rushed at Coke and grabbed him at the shoulders.

"Don't shoot!" a policeman shouted. "They're too close together! You might hit the boy!"

Coke and Dr. Warsaw grabbed hold of each other and started wrestling on the cable. One slip, they both knew, and one or both of them would fall to their death.

"Watch out!" Pep shouted.

"Be careful, Coke!" hollered Mrs. McDonald.

"I'm warning you," Coke told Dr. Warsaw. "I studied karate for five years. I have a brown belt."

"Oh, so you flunked your black belt test, eh?" Dr. Warsaw said, taunting the boy.

In fact, Coke *had* flunked his black belt test. Twice. And he wasn't happy about it. Angered, he shoved Dr. Warsaw away to give himself a couple of feet of space.

"Meet the Inflictor!" Coke shouted.

Then he spun around, swept his right leg sideways, and kicked Dr. Warsaw's legs out from under him. The older man screamed as his butt slammed against the main cable. He reached out and grabbed for something to hold on to, but the surface of the cable was smooth.

"Noooooooooo!" he screamed as he slid off and dropped out of sight.

Dr. Warsaw was gone.

EPILOGUE

They never heard the splash. By the time everyone had rushed to the railing and peered down into the murky water, it was too late. Dr. Warsaw's body did not come back to the surface. They never found it. It may have washed out to sea or been eaten by sharks.

Some people on the bridge that day cried. Those were the people who didn't know Dr. Warsaw and all the evil things he had done. Those who *did* know him just felt a sense of relief. It was better this way. A quick but painful death had to be preferable to spending the rest of his life in prison.

Nobody felt more relieved than Coke and Pep. Their summer-long cross-country nightmare was finally over. When Coke climbed down off the cable, there was no applause or cheering from the crowd. A man had died. Pep embraced Coke and their parents held on to the two of them like they would never let go. When they finally did, Mya and

Bones came over for a group hug.

"It's over," Mya said quietly. "Dr. Warsaw will never bother you again."

"We're sorry about all the things you kids went through this summer," said Bones. "We tried our best to protect you."

"I know," Pep said. "We wouldn't be alive right now if it weren't for you."

"We'll never forget you," Coke said, sniffling.

The twins were about to walk away when another group of people approached—Mrs. Higgins, John Pain, and the bowler dudes. Instinctively, Coke and Pep backed away and prepared to make a run for it. But instead of attacking, the bowler dudes threw their arms around them.

"We'll miss you kids," said the clean-shaven bowler dude, tears running down his cheeks.

"In a strange way," Coke replied, "I'm going to miss you, too."

"It was fun trying to kill you," said the mustachioed bowler dude.

Mrs. Higgins moved in for a hug and told the twins she would see them when school started in September. They thanked her for saving their lives in Death Valley, and driving them back to San Francisco.

"Let's blow this pop stand," Coke told his sister.

They would have to give a statement to the police, of course. And there was still the matter of getting home and returning to a normal, teenage life after all they had been through. That might take some getting used to. But The Genius Files program was over. With Dr. Warsaw out of the picture, Coke and Pep would never again have to worry about lunatics chasing them around and trying to kill them at any opportunity.

"You two were *amazing*!" Mrs. McDonald said, still reluctant to let go of her children.

"Now let me get this straight," said Dr. McDonald. "That Warsaw guy has been chasing you ever since we left home?"

"Yes!" Pep said. "That's what we've been trying to tell you all along!"

"We just thought you were putting us on," Mrs. McDonald said. "You know, the way teenagers do."

"It was all real, Mom," Coke explained. "At first we didn't want to worry you. Then, when we decided to tell you the truth, you wouldn't believe us. But we've been almost frozen to death, boiled in oil, pushed into a sand pit—"

"Thrown into a vat of Spam, kidnapped, blasted with loud music—" added Pep.

"—swarmed by bats, abducted by aliens, sprayed

with poison gas, had stuff dropped on our heads . . . ," said Coke.

"And all of these things actually happened?" asked Dr. McDonald. "You didn't make *any* of it up?"

"Yes, it all happened!" Pep shouted at him. "And a lot of other stuff, too. You could fill a—"

"Book!" Dr. McDonald said, his eyes suddenly wide. "This is it! This is the idea I've been searching for! I can write a novel about two kids who travel cross-country while some bad guys are trying to kill them the whole time! And their parents don't know a thing about it! It can't miss! This could be my best-seller!"

"That's a *great* idea, Dad!" said Pep. "We'll tell you exactly what happened."

"Ben, I don't know if it's a good idea to put your name on that book," said Mrs. McDonald. "How will the university feel if one of their respected professors publishes a crazy novel like that? You could lose your job."

"You may be right, Bridge."

"What if you used a pen name, Dad?" Pep suggested. "Then nobody would know it was you."

After some discussion, Dr. McDonald came up with a pen name. Coke and Pep told their father everything that had happened to them since they started the trip.

There was so much information that he was able to make it into a five-book series, which he called the Genius Files. And guess what happened after the first book was published?

The New York Times

Book Review

Print | Children's Best Sellers   SALES PERIOD OF JANUARY 29-FEBRUARY 4

THIS WEEK	PAPERBACK BOOKS	WEEKS ON LIST
1	**THE BOOK THIEF,** by Markus Zusak. (Knopf, $12.99.) A girl saves books from Nazi burning. (Ages 14 and up)	230
2	**WAR HORSE,** by Michael Morpurgo. (Scholastic, $8.99.) A half-Thoroughbred farm horse is taken from his owner for battle in 1914. (Ages 14 and up)	13
3	**THIRTEEN REASONS WHY,** by Jay Asher. (Razorbill, $10.99.) Before she commits suicide, a girl sends recordings to 13 people. (Ages 12 and up)	34
4	**THE GENIUS FILES: MISSION UNSTOPPABLE,** by Dan Gutman. (HarperCollins, $6.99.) Twelve-year-old twins are part of a top-secret government organization. (Ages 8 to12)	2
5	**SWITCHED,** by Amanda Hocking. (St. Martin's Griffin, $8.99.) In the first book in the Trylle trilogy, an emotionally damaged high school girl realizes she may not be human. (Ages 12 and up)	5
6	**THE RED PYRAMID,** by Rick Riordan. (Disney-Hyperion, $9.99.) Ancient gods (this time from Egypt) and a mortal family meet. (Ages 10 and up)	25
7	**CLOCKWORK ANGEL,** by Cassandra Clare. (Margaret K. McElderry, $10.99.) Victorian England proves a treacherous place. (Ages 14 and up)	18
8	**MATCHED,** by Ally Condie. (Speak, $9.99.) In this dystopian romance, a girl rebels. (Ages 12 and up)	20
9	**I AM NUMBER FOUR,** by Pittacus Lore. (HarperCollins, $9.99.) Members of another civilization live secretly on Earth. (Ages 14 and up)	24
10	**BEFORE I FALL,** by Lauren Oliver. (Harper/HarperCollins, $9.99.) Last kisses, death and second chances await a teenager one fateful Friday. (Ages 14 and up)	6

ABOUT THE PHOTOS

Most of the photographs in this book were taken by Dan Gutman, or created by Nina Wallace (Dan's wife). But for three photos, we must give credit where credit is due. The photos of the earth on page 50 and the moon on page 55 are from NASA. The image of radio telescopes on page 95 is courtesy of NRAO/AUI.

ABOUT THE AUTHOR

Dan Gutman is the pen name of Dr. Benjamin McDonald, history professor at San Francisco State University. Any resemblance between him and the children's book author of the same name is purely coincidental. But if you would like to find out about Dan Gutman and his books, go to www.dangutman.com.